RIVER OF THE WOLVES

RIVER of the WOLVES

by STEPHEN W. MEADER

ILLUSTRATED BY EDWARD SHENTON

SOUTHERN SKIES

SOUTHERN SKIES
LITTLE ROCK, ARKANSAS
www.southernskies.com

Dedication

The republication of this book is dedicated with love to Jackson Farrow, Jr.---great friend, trusted advisor, attorney extraordinaire---by Jerry Atchley

LIST OF ILLUSTRATIONS

FOREWORD

WHEN I was a boy in New Hampshire it was my good fortune to have numerous uncles and aunts who were able story-tellers. The tales they told had been handed down through generations of my family who had lived in the neighborhood for almost 300 years.

All through the pattern of those stories ran mentions of Canada. The very name sent delightful shivers up and down my back. Canada—so close and yet so vast and dark and mysterious.

I played daily with the sons of French Canadian mill hands and wood choppers, and a jolly, spirited crew they were. But they had little to do with the Canada of the old tales—the Canada of wolves and Indians.

It was Aunt Julia who told me about our ancestress, the grim Hannah Dustin, who escaped from her red-skinned captors on their way to Canada, after the Haverhill massacre. She came home with the scalps of the ten Indians she had killed in the process, and I was even shown the ancient stains on the blanket in which she wrapped her grisly souvenirs.

Uncle Valentine unfolded the tale of the hard winter, back in the sixties, when most of the menfolks were off to war and the wolves came down from Canada. They slaughtered the sheep in their pens, harried the cattle and drifted like gray shadows along the three miles of snowy road that the children walked to school.

There was Uncle John's story about Canada Billy, too. Uncle John was only a lad when he accompanied Grandfather Meader north to Quebec to buy a horse. They drove in a buggy, taking a week each way, and the thrill of that experience was still in my uncle's eyes fifty years after. Canada Billy was the name

vii

of the horse they purchased. He was a Canada "chunk"—a short-coupled, powerful draft animal whose gentleness, wisdom and ability to pull were never equaled, according to Uncle John.

Most thrilling of all were visits I made with Father to the spot where the old Meader garrison had stood, on Dover Point. Sitting on the green mound which was all that remained of the log fort, he told me the legend of the Cocheco massacre, handed down from generation to generation in our family.

The Dover settlement, then known as Cocheco, was under the command of a hard-headed soldier and trader named Major Waldron. He had little use for the Indians except to cheat them out of their furs. In 1676 this gentleman invited a large party of Penacooks to a feast. The tribe was at peace with the settlers. They came to the town unarmed and unsuspecting, and by a cruel ruse Major Waldron had them crowd together in the village square. Suddenly they found themselves looking into the mouth of a loaded cannon, ringed about by armed soldiers. Four hundred were taken prisoner. Those not put to death were sold into slavery in the West Indies. Only a handful escaped.

More than twelve years later the remnant of the Penacooks, led by their chief, Kankamaugus, got their revenge.

On the evening of the 27th of June, 1689, Indian squaws came to the various garrisons in the settlement, humbly asking shelter for the night. One or two of them were admitted to each of the five scattered block-houses. Some time before dawn the squaws rose silently and opened the barred doors. Indian braves rushed in to overpower the sleeping settlers. More than fifty colonists were killed or carried off as captives that night. The 80-year-old Major Waldron was one of the victims, and they taunted and tortured him before his death.

For almost a century Northern New England lay under the dread shadow of Indian attack. Usually the savages came in summer, stealing out of the woods to burn lonely homesteads.

Sometimes they raided in the dead of winter, as in the terrible snowshoe war of 1704. But always, egged on by their French masters, it was out of Canada that they came.

Perhaps that is why a New Hampshire boy, born many generations after the last scalp was lifted, still feels that spine-tingling chill when he thinks of the Dominion to the north.

S. W. M.

RIVER OF THE WOLVES

I

THE BOY stopped in the shade of a big pine and wiped his dripping forehead with the sleeve of his shirt. He was tall and strong for a fifteen-year-old, but four days of tramping under a July sun had sweated all the fat off him. The sturdy cowhide shoes in which he had set out were so worn now that he could feel every pebble through their soles.

The last wagon road lay a dozen miles behind him. Since he left the Merrimack River he had been following a rough trail up across the hills. But it wasn't the hard going that worried him. It was the fact that his food was gone. The last apple, the last bit of ham and dry loaf-end of bread in his pack had been eaten for breakfast that morning. If he didn't reach his uncle's soon he would have to beg a meal.

A red squirrel in the pine tree overhead began chattering in a new key, different from the half-hearted scolding that had been going on for some minutes. The boy listened.

From somewhere down the trail came the faint clink of a horseshoe on a stone. He waited and after a little while the traveler appeared. It was a tall, gray-bearded man, afoot, leading a sorry-looking little nag. Tied on the animal's back were two sacks of meal.

The man looked up and nodded. "Nice day," he remarked through his whiskers. "Ye look sort o' tuckered, son. Been far?"

The boy grinned. "Dover," he replied. "Close to seventy miles, I guess. Maybe you can tell me how much farther it is to the Contoocook. I'm looking for Jedediah Foster's place. I'm his nephew, Dave Foster."

"Wal, now," the man replied, "that's interestin'. Yer uncle's a nigh neighbor o' mine—couple o' miles north. My name's Andy McClure. Jest come along with me an' I'll git ye there 'fore suppertime. Jed said he was expectin' ye."

Dave settled the straps of his pack, empty now except for his spare shirts and underwear, and fell in beside the long-striding farmer.

"Been down to the gristmill to git some corn ground," McClure explained. "Left 'fore daylight this mornin'."

He looked the boy over with an appraising eye. "Jed can use a good hand," he said. "He's got most of his hayin' done, but the corn needs hoein'. Plan to stay the rest o' the summer?"

"Yes," answered Dave. "Till September anyway. I'll have to go back to school then."

They climbed steadily for another mile. Then the trail

4

crossed a hilltop and suddenly they looked off across miles of wooded valley and meadowland.

"That's the Contoocook intervale," McClure volunteered. "Pretty country, ain't it? We raise some good crops in them rich bottoms, too. Summers when the Injuns leave us alone, that is."

"Have there been any Indians around this year?" Dave asked.

The farmer's eyes narrowed and his face was grim. "Nope," he said. "Leastways, not yet. They burned me out three years ago. Might be a raid any time, only the French have got most of 'em fightin' over Ticonderoga way."

The woods closed in on the trail again as they started down the hill, and they moved through a cool, green alley of shade. McClure's words had made Dave realize that for the first time in his life he was in Indian country. He stole a furtive glance into the forest, half expecting to see a copper-skinned savage skulking there in the shadows.

The next moment he was ashamed of the idea, for McClure walked along in complete unconcern. The lanky farmer wasn't even armed.

Dave asked him about that. "Don't you folks back here generally carry a gun?" he inquired. "If you should see a deer, I mean—wouldn't you want to shoot it?"

"Meat ain't so good this time o' year," McClure replied. "We wait till fall an' lay us in a store o' venison. It needs to be hung a spell, an' we can keep it better in cold weather. As fer the gun, I leave that home when I have to go to mill. My ole woman can handle it, an' I'd rather have her ready fer trouble if the Injuns should come."

They went on through the warm afternoon. The sun was still high when they came to a good-sized clearing beside the river.

"This is my place," said McClure. "Ye'll notice the house is built with an overhang—blockhouse style. After the last raid I decided we'd better have a garrison house where the neighbors could run to if there was trouble. We'd like to have ye drop in a spell, but I s'pose ye'll want to be goin' along to Jed's."

"Thanks," Dave told him. "I'd like to stop and pay you a call, but right now I'm anxious to get there."

The bearded farmer pointed to the farther edge of the clearing. "Trail's right over yonder," said he. "Keep goin' an' ye'll be at yer uncle's in a couple o' shakes."

Dave crossed the clearing between rows of sturdy, waist-high corn, and plunged into the woods once more. The "couple of shakes" mentioned by McClure turned out to be a half hour of steady walking. At the end of that time, however, he came out of the pines into a natural meadow by the river bank. The stubble showed where hay had recently been cut. Beyond the meadow stood a little log house and barn, and there was a good-sized cornfield between the buildings and the edge of the woods.

He hurried forward, watching the open door of the cabin. It had been four years since he saw his uncle, and he had done a lot of growing in that time. He wondered if

BEYOND THE MEADOW STOOD A LITTLE LOG HOUSE AND BARN

he would be recognized.

There was a sudden bark from behind the house and a lean black and tan hound came trotting around the corner. It caught sight of the boy and halted, barking more loudly. Then a female figure appeared in the doorway. At the same moment a big, red-haired man came out of the barn with a pitchfork in his hand.

"Uncle Jed!" Dave shouted. "Don't you know me? I'm here at last."

"Why, it must be David!" exclaimed the woman, shading her eyes to peer at him.

A wide grin overspread the man's sunburned face.

"Be still, you, Monk!" he told the hound. "This is Dave— he's goin' to be a friend o' yours."

He strode forward and greeted the boy with a powerful handclasp. "Sort o' hoped you'd get here today," said he. "How are you—played out?"

"No," laughed Dave. "My shoes are 'most worn through but I'm ready to start hoeing right this minute."

"Indeed, you won't do any such thing," the woman in the doorway told him. "Come in here and let's get acquainted. I'm your Aunt Maria."

She was a plump, vivacious little lady, with dark hair and snapping black eyes. Dave liked her immediately. She was a good housekeeper, too, as he could see the moment he entered the cabin.

The furnishings were plain, and most of them home-made, but the floor was swept clean and everything was as neat as a pin. One square room filled the whole of the little log structure. A door at one side opened into a lean-to which served as a bedroom, and there was a ladder in the corner leading to the loft. A giant stone fireplace filled one whole wall.

There was a long iron crane hinged to the left wall of the fireplace, and on it hung a blackened pot. Other pans and skillets of iron and copper were ranged on the wall. Half a dozen precious blue china plates stood in splendor in the corner cupboard. A spinning wheel, a puncheon table and three or four split hickory chairs made up the rest of the room's furniture.

"It's been so hot," said Aunt Maria, "I thought I wouldn't build a supper fire. But there's plenty of cold buttermilk in the spring, and blueberries, and a whole crock of fresh-made doughnuts. Think that'll hold you? I'll get it ready while Jed shows you 'round the place."

Dave followed his uncle out to the log barn. In the stalls were a pair of placid-looking oxen, a red cow and a calf. The new-cut hay was piled in a tall stack outside. And behind the barn was a pen containing a big black and white sow and a litter of six pigs.

"We're pretty well fixed here, as you can see," his uncle told him proudly. "We don't miss the town fol-de-rols as much as you'd think. This land here is some o' the best in the Hampshire Grants. We can raise about anything we need. Soon as I get a few sheep we'll have wool, too."

He pointed off across the clearing. "Look at that corn,"

he said. "Didn't get it planted till 'most the middle o' June, an' it's higher'n a three-rail fence now. After the crops are in I aim to cut an' burn another ten acres off the edge o' the woods. An' next year I want to plant a few apple trees. Then I won't have to take off my hat to anybody—not the King's Governor himself!"

The spring was fifty yards north of the cabin—a clear, deep pool with water bubbling up from its sandy bottom. It was protected by a pole lean-to that kept out sun and stray leaves. Deep in its coolness stood an earthenware crock of buttermilk, which they took with them to the house.

While supper was being eaten, Dave described his trip. There were many questions for him to answer—about his family in Dover—about the preparations for Lord Amherst's expedition against Louisburg—and about the prices and styles of millinery in the coast towns. These last inquiries came, of course, from Aunt Maria, and the boy could give her very little information.

Uncle Jed told the meager news of the frontier settlements. There had been a raid by a small band of Indians—Hurons and Penacooks—over toward the Connecticut early in the spring. Two women and a child were killed but some white men from Number Four had overtaken the war party and brought home half a dozen scalps.

"The story is now," Dave's uncle concluded, "that the French have called in all the tribes an' sent 'em against General Abercrombie. So unless he gets licked at Ticonderoga we'll probably be able to work in peace the rest o' the summer."

"I hope you're right," said Dave. "I'd sort of like to see a real Indian, though. All we've got around Dover are a few old drunks that come to the door selling baskets."

"Well, they'd better not come here—the nasty things," Aunt Maria remarked with a toss of her head. "I know how to fire the gun and I wouldn't hesitate a second."

Dave mentioned McClure's blockhouse. "Have you had to use it yet?" he asked.

Jed Foster laughed good-naturedly. "Old Andy McClure don't trust the Injuns since his cabin was burned," said he. "He's a mite over-careful now, but we humor him. I doubt if we'll ever have to run to the garrison."

"Just the same," his wife reproved him, "it pays to be careful. You know I've always been at you to get an extra gun besides the one you take to the field with you."

"I know," Jed replied. "If I have any cash over this fall, I'll think about tradin' for one."

Dave went out with his uncle to do the evening chores. There was a bend of the Contoocook a short distance from the barn, and while Jed was milking, the boy drove the oxen down to the river to drink. Monk, the hound, had accepted him as a part of the family. Unlike most of his breed, Monk was a fair herd dog, and he kept the big beasts from straying on the way home.

Just before they reached the barn door, Dave saw something moving above the green of the corn, far over toward the woods. Monk must have caught the scent at the same time, for he was off into the cornfield like a black and tan streak. Watching, the boy saw a deer lift her head, the big ears forming a "V." Then, as Monk gave voice in a deep, musical bay, the doe turned lightly and vanished among the trees.

"Shucks!" said Uncle Jed. "Once he gets to runnin' a deer he's liable to be out all night."

They sat on the doorstep in the dusk and listened to the distant bugling of the hound, sometimes clear on the night breeze, sometimes so faint they could hardly hear it.

"Well," Aunt Maria told them at last, "we'd better go to bed if we want to save a candle. You men folks'll want to be in the fields early, I expect."

Dave climbed the ladder to the loft, stripped off his clothes and lay down on the straw pallet. It was hot up there under the roof, but the boy was tired enough to sleep. Almost before he knew it, morning had come, and he could hear the clink of pots and pans from the room below. Quickly he pulled on his shirt and butternut breeches and scrambled down the ladder.

Within half an hour Dave and his uncle had done the morning chores. The cow had been milked, the pigs fed, and the cattle turned out into a little brush-fenced pasture in the meadow by the river.

At breakfast Uncle Jed planned the day's work. There was a pile of birch logs to be split into kindling before they started to hoe corn. The farmer looked at Dave's bare feet and grinned.

"Got rid o' those shoes, did you?" he remarked. "I liked to go barefoot myself when I was your age. It's all right around the place, here, but you'll need something more when we go in the woods after berries an' such. I'll fix you up a pair o' reg'lar Injun moccasins. Got some hide left from the moose I killed last winter an' it's good, tough leather. Here—let's see the shape o' your soles."

He took a bit of charred wood from the hearth and traced the outline of each of Dave's feet on the puncheon floor.

"Now, Maria," he told his wife with a twinkle, "don't you go scrubbin' those marks off till I get the boy's moccasins made."

Monk, the hound, had come limping in before daylight and lay exhausted in the shade behind the house, watching Dave and his uncle split kindling.

"How far do you reckon he traveled?" asked the boy.

"Can't say," Uncle Jed replied. "Prob'ly thirty or forty miles. Never did catch up with that deer, though. He was mighty hungry when he got home."

They stacked the firewood in a neat pile under the eaves and Jed Foster looked eastward at the sun.

"Must be towards eight o'clock already," said he. "Can't waste the day like this. You take the jug, Dave, an' fill her up with spring water. I'll go fetch the hoes an' we'll get to work."

II

OEING corn was a job Dave disliked as much as any boy of his age. It was hard, hot, back-breaking work but it was one of the necessary evils of farm life. He had done enough of it in the family's corn patch in Dover to be fairly competent. However, he found he had to hustle to keep even close to his uncle. The big red-haired man was fast and tireless.

Dave had never worked in finer soil. The alluvial earth of the bottom-lands was dark and rich, and contained fewer stones than most New Hampshire ground. It grew magnificent corn, but the weeds flourished, too. Cutting them out cleanly with the hoe blade was laborious work.

At the end of an hour Dave was a full half-row behind. His uncle looked back at him and chuckled.

"Don't kill yourself tryin' to keep up, lad," he said. "You'll get blisters 'fore you get calluses if you work too hard. Here—let's take a breather and get us a drink."

They went over to the shade of the woods where Dave had left the jug and sat down for a rest.

"Tell me some more about the Indians," said the boy. "Last night you said it was Hurons and Penacooks that made the raid in the spring. Do they both come from Canada?"

"Well, it's this way," the older man explained. "The Hurons always did live up there. They've been helpin' the French for more'n a hundred years, I reckon. Some of 'em talk French as good as they do Injun. But there's half a dozen tribes that used to hunt this country, an' they're the ones that like to come back here scalpin' an' burnin'. When we chased 'em out o' New England they moved up along the St. Lawrence an' the French gave 'em villages an' priests. You've heard o' the St. Francis Injuns? They're all from down this way—Penobscots and Norridgewocks from Maine—Assagunticooks from the Androscoggin country—Pequawkets from the Saco, an' Penacooks from the Merrimack. All of 'em speak the same language—Abenaki. That's why some folks call 'em the Abenaki tribes."

He took another long swig from the water jug.

"St. Francis is just one o' their towns," he went on. "There's another at Beçancour an' one on the Chaudière, a little ways from Quebec. Prob'ly more, too, that I never heard of. What are you so interested in Injuns for, Dave? Not scared, are you?"

"Gosh, no!" said the boy scornfully. "I just wondered, that's all. When I'm old enough I'd like to join up with

Rogers' Rangers and help wipe out the Injuns for keeps."

"Hm," Jed Foster mused. "You'd have to be a pretty good man in the woods. I used to know Bob Rogers, back in Portsmouth. He can figger out a trail as good as any Injun, an' he's twice as much man—strong as a bull. I bet he's taken fifty scalps in the last five years. With the bounty at forty pounds apiece he must be rich. If I was a youngster, though, I don't know's I'd pick him for a leader. He's a wild, crazy devil an' some day he'll push his luck too far."

He got up and stretched his big arms. "What say, boy?" he asked. "Ready to tackle that hoein' again?"

.   .   .   .

By the end of Dave's first week on the Contoocook he was as brown and almost as hard as his uncle. The calluses on his palms were smooth and thick as sole leather, and his feet had toughened from going barefoot.

Four days of steady hoeing had finished the big cornfield. Then the heat was broken by a northeast storm and they were kept indoors. That was when Uncle Jed made the moccasins. He cut the tanned moose-skin carefully, punched holes in the proper places with an awl and sewed each moccasin up with thin strips of rawhide. When Dave tried them on they felt more comfortable than any shoes he had ever worn. The leather was soft and pliable and, thanks to the pattern Uncle Jed had made of his feet, they were a perfect fit.

Aunt Maria looked out the cabin door that evening and announced that she could see a star between the clouds.

"The weather's clearing," she said. "If it's a fair day tomorrow I'd like to go down to McClures'. I've got some quilting to do and I can use Mrs. McClure's frame."

Uncle Jed laughed. "That's right," he replied. "An' you can enjoy a little female gossip at the same time. You go right ahead, Maria. Dave an' I'll make out fine. I've got some fences to mend. Now you've got your moccasins, Dave, you might go an' get us some blueberries. I won't be needin' you tomorrow."

"Sure," said the boy. "I always liked picking berries. Where's the best place?"

"You'll find 'em most anywhere, but there's a hill a couple o' miles to the west where the woods burned a few years back. They're plenty thick there. I've blazed a trail to the patch, so you can find it easy enough."

When the sun rose next morning, Dave had already been up for an hour. He raced through the morning chores and before breakfast he had cut a broad strip of bark from a canoe birch by the river. It took him only a few minutes to fashion it into a basket big enough to hold five or six quarts of berries. He fastened it together with sharpened green twigs and braided a handle of willow shoots.

"I'll take your Aunt Maria down to McClures'," his uncle told him at breakfast. "You can carry along some bread an' cheese an' stay out all day if you want. I won't look for you till evenin' chore time."

That was just what Dave had hoped for. After his enforced idleness during the storm, he was looking forward to a day in the woods. He packed a crisp half-loaf of his aunt's good bread and a slab of homemade cheese in the bark basket and was ready to start.

It was a fine morning, clear and fresh after the rain. As Dave crossed the cornfield he heard Aunt Maria calling a cheery farewell. He turned and waved. Jed Foster and his wife were walking south along the river trail—the tall, red-haired farmer and the little feminine figure in the gay calico dress. For a moment they were in bright sunshine against the green of trees. Then they passed into the shadows and Dave shivered—he didn't know why. It was as if a sudden cloud had crossed the sun, making the day chilly. Yet when he looked upward the sky was blue and cloudless.

He shook himself, grinned a bit sheepishly, and went on toward the edge of the forest. Somewhere ahead, high up among the pine tops, a whitethroat sang plaintively. "Old Sam Peabody-Peabody-Peabody"—that was how New England boys interpreted the rising series of notes. In a moment Dave had found the blazed tree that marked the beginning of the trail and plunged eagerly into the woods. His uncle's blazes were not hard to follow and there was little undergrowth to hold him back. He reached the burned-over hillside in less than an hour.

It was a mournful-looking piece of country. A few gaunt, blackened trunks of pine trees stood up starkly in a waste of low-growing brush. But the blueberries were there. The boy's eyes opened wide at the sight of the first bush. Its branches drooped under the weight of misty-blue fruit.

Dave took the bread and cheese out of his basket and set to work, stripping whole handfuls of ripe berries from each spray. He kept no track of the time but picked steadily till the berries fairly overflowed the basket's sides. When he could carry no more without spilling them, he looked at the sun and saw that it was still an hour before noon.

Perhaps he could make himself another basket. The only birches in sight on the burned hillside were saplings hardly as big as his wrist. He angled upward toward the crest, looking for a tree that would suit his purpose, and came at length to a rocky ridge that must have served as a fire-break. Beyond it the big pines began again, live and green. He was high enough here to command a view of the country to the north and east. The folds of dark, forest-covered hills reached away mile after mile till they were blue in the distance. And above them, farther still, loomed the White Mountains, capped by one snowy peak, higher than the rest.

He sat down on the granite ledge and looked long at the ranges, wondering if that biggest mountain had a name. By now he was beginning to be hungry. Bread and cheese would be dry fare without water, and he decided to find a brook or a spring if possible.

Going down the other side of the ridge, he hung the basket of blueberries on a pine limb in a shady spot, took his bearings so that he could find the place again, and started into the woods.

The hill was steep and fallen trees and underbrush made the going difficult. However, he could see that he was de-

WHEN HE WAS BENDING TO DRINK HE SAW THE MARK ON THE
OTHER SIDE OF THE BROOK

scending into some sort of ravine, at the bottom of which he might expect to find a watercourse. Sure enough, after a few minutes he looked down through the evergreen boughs and caught sight of a narrow stream-bed where a tiny rivulet flowed between moss-covered stones.

Clutching his packet of food he slid down the bank, knelt on hands and knees and thrust his face down into the cold, clear water. When his thirst was satisfied, he sat back to enjoy his lunch. It was when he had eaten the last of the bread and cheese and was bending to drink again that he saw the mark in the soft moss on the other side of the brook. The moccasin track was clear and fresh. It had been made since yesterday's rain.

Dave had a creepy feeling as he stared at it. He had not crossed the stream. Somebody else had left that print—somebody with a foot a little larger than his own. He stood up cautiously, looking down the ravine and listening. A noonday hush hung over the forest. No birds sang, and no breeze stirred the pine boughs overhead. If a twig had snapped anywhere within a quarter of a mile the boy thought he could hear it.

At the end of a minute or two his tenseness left him and he stepped silently across the brook for a closer look at the footprint. The toe was pointed downstream. Dave moved along the bank for fifty yards without finding any other sign.

After all, he told himself, there was no real reason for him to be disturbed. The track might have been made by any of a dozen settlers from the Contoocook, or by some roving hunter. Indian moccasins were worn by many of the backwoodsmen of the region, Uncle Jed had told him.

In spite of all his efforts to reassure himself, the boy had an uneasy feeling as he turned back up the stream. As quietly as possible he climbed the side of the ravine and made his way toward the rocky crest above the pines. His basket of berries hung undisturbed where he had left it.

Somehow the pleasure had gone out of his day's excursion. He no longer thought of making another basket or picking more blueberries. He wanted to get back to his uncle's clearing.

With one furtive glance over his shoulder at the forest, he picked up the bark basket and started down the hill through the blueberry thickets. Dotted over the waste were clumps of small jack-pine—new growth that had started since the fire. Just as he drew abreast of one of these a sudden roar startled him so that he spilled nearly half his berries. It was a pair of ruffed grouse that had flown out of the pine clump with a thunder of wings.

Angry at himself, he stopped and picked more fruit to replace what he had lost. But the urge to get home was still in the back of his mind. As soon as the basket was filled again he set out for the place where he thought he had entered the burn.

He sighted a dead pine stub he had picked out as a landmark and went confidently toward the edge of the woods. When he got there something seemed to have gone wrong.

There was no blazed tree marking the beginning of the trail.

Uncertainly he looked back and realized that there were dozens of those blackened pine trunks, and all of them looked very much alike. Dave was ashamed of his wood-craft and exasperated by the delay, for it was now well along in the afternoon. He searched the border of the burn, first north, then south, and still found no blazes. At last he decided to strike through the woods, trail or no trail.

There was enough sun, even in the thick of the forest, to enable him to keep his direction fairly well. But the deeper he went into the woods the more obstacles seemed to block his path. First he had to make his way around a blow-down of dead timber. Then he got entangled in a dense spruce thicket. And after more than an hour of dogged travel he found himself in a swamp where water stood among the tree roots and black mud sucked at his moccasins.

Wearily he backed off to higher ground, took his bearings once more by the low sun and circled half a mile to the north to get around the swamp. Suddenly, right in front of him, was the familiar ax-mark of a blaze. He had stumbled on the trail after all his wanderings.

From that point it was a matter of only a few minutes' walk to the clearing, and he trudged along more cheerfully. When he came out of the woods the golden light of late afternoon lay over the fields. He looked about for his uncle and saw him working on a snake fence that separated the pasture from the corn patch.

"Hi!" he called. "Look at the berries I got, Uncle Jed."

The tall farmer straightened up and wiped his brow.

"Good enough!" said he. "Better take 'em over to the house. Your aunt'll be glad to see those when she comes back. She's stayin' the night at McClures'."

He swung his ax two or three times on the pole he was trimming, then looked up again. "Didn't have any trouble findin' the place, I guess," he said with a grin.

"No," Dave told him. "No, I—I found it all right." He was ashamed to say anything about the trip home, and his worry about the moccasin track seemed silly now.

He turned toward the cabin. "If you're going to work a while," he said, "I'll bring you a drink from the spring."

Monk, the hound, rose from his resting place by the barn door and greeted him with a wag of his tail. He followed the boy into the kitchen and over to the spring. As Dave was filling the jug with water he heard the dog growl behind him. Quickly he turned his head. Above the waist-high corn he saw shadowy figures—two—three—half a dozen of them—racing toward the house.

FOR A second or two the boy crouched there, stunned by the suddenness of the attack. Then he sprang erect.

"Uncle Jed!" he yelled with desperate urgency. "Uncle Jed—Injuns!"

He saw the farmer pause in the middle of an ax-stroke and turn to look where he was pointing. Uncle Jed snatched up something from the ground and Dave saw it was his gun. The red-haired man was running now in long, galloping strides, trying to reach the buildings ahead of the Indians.

Monk had disappeared. But the boy heard a deep, half-strangled bark in the cornfield and saw one of the leading savages whirl and strike downward with his tomahawk. After that the hound's voice was still. Poor, brave old Monk!

The moment's delay allowed Jed Foster to gain on the attackers. He was almost to the barn when a gunshot roared across the clearing. Horrified, Dave saw his uncle stumble and pitch forward, his musket flying out of his hands.

Instinctively the boy had started toward the house, still carrying the full jug. Now he stopped. Half hidden by the weeds and bushes along the path, he watched in helpless rage while a copper-skinned warrior swooped down on the prostrate man, brandishing a scalping knife. He wanted desperately to aid the fallen man but he had no weapon, no skill to match those crafty fighters. As the knife flashed downward it was more than he could bear to see. Sick at heart he turned and fled, dropping the jug and bending low in an effort to get to the woods beyond the spring without being seen. He ran blindly, knowing only that Uncle Jed would want him to save himself if he could.

There was no noise of pursuit behind him when he reached the cover of the alder thicket. Brush grew dense and high there along the river. He had to crawl on his belly to get under the interlacing branches. Only after he had penetrated the thicket for a dozen yards did he stop and lie still, listening.

The sounds that came to him were distant and confused. Several times he heard high-pitched shouts that must be Indian war whoops! There was a frightened bellowing of cattle and once the squeal of the old sow rose above the other noises and ended suddenly in a grunting gurgle.

He could see almost nothing from his hiding place, but he was aware, after a while, that the gathering darkness had a queer red tinge. Then the smell of smoke drifted his way.

DAVE SAW HIS UNCLE STUMBLE—HIS MUSKET FLYING OUT OF
HIS HANDS

They had fired the haystack and the buildings.

Tears of grief and rage misted the boy's eyes. He wiped them away fiercely and prayed as he had never prayed before. He prayed for the safety of his aunt, down at the McClure blockhouse, and he prayed for his own deliverance or, if he was to be taken, for strength to bear the torture.

He was calmer after that, and able to think more clearly. This place he had run to in his panic was far from safe, as he began to realize.

The war party had surely seen him when he shouted the warning to his uncle. They knew he had been at the spring, and the first place they would hunt him was here, in the nearest cover. Up to now they had been too busy looting the premises, slaughtering the stock and burning the buildings to come after him. But if he hoped to get away he had no time to lose.

Creeping on hands and knees he worked westward, away from the river. If he could get free of the thicket and into the big timber on higher ground he might put some distance between himself and the horror back there in the clearing.

There was enough light from the evening sky and the blazing haystack to show him that he was almost out of the alders. Pushing aside the last low-growing boughs, he stood up, drawing a deep breath. Just ahead, the red glow flickered on big pine trunks. He was in the real woods now, and there was room to run.

But before he had taken three strides he knew his escape

was cut off. From behind the trees two Indians leaped out of hiding. The nearest one was only yards away. Dave had a glimpse of a lithe red body, naked except for the loin-cloth—a snarling face, ghastly with its stripes of black and white war paint—and a lifted hand that clutched a toma-hawk. He didn't wait for the blow to fall. Gritting his teeth he dove straight for the Indian's legs. They were slippery with some kind of grease, but he seized them in both arms, ramming his shoulder into his antagonist's stomach. The Indian's breath went out of him in a surprised grunt. The next second Dave was on top of him, grappling desperately for the hatchet.

He had the savage's wrist pinned to the earth when something hit him on the back of the head and his mind blacked out in a whirl of stars.

It must have been several minutes before Dave regained consciousness. He was lying on his side, his hands bound behind him, and it was pitch dark in the woods. Through the painful pounding in his head he could hear two voices muttering. The Indian words were unintelligible, but from their tones he gathered that an argument was going on. That might explain why he was still alive. One of the braves —probably the one he had downed—was angrily demanding his scalp. But there was a note of authority in the other's voice that gave the boy a ray of hope.

As his eyes became adjusted to the night he could see the outlines of their bodies against the faint glow that still came from the clearing. They were slim and young, he realized—boys only a little older than himself. This must be their first expedition against the settlements.

At length the pair seemed to reach some sort of an agreement. They came over to him and one of them poked him in the back with the shaft of a tomahawk. There was a guttural command that he took for an order to get up. Clumsily he rolled over, pulled his knees under him and rose to his feet, swaying with dizziness.

One of the young braves led the way toward the edge of the clearing while the other pushed Dave on from the rear.

Other dark forms came loping through the corn to join them at the border of the woods. Some carried chunks of bloody meat. Others had bundles of loot—a copper kettle—pewter spoons—one of Aunt Maria's bombazine gowns. There were seven men in all. The newcomers scowled at Dave and jabbered in low voices.

They stayed there only a moment. The tallest member of the party, who seemed to be their leader, waved his arm impatiently and beckoned them into the forest. They went at a fast pace in spite of the darkness.

Dave's head was clearer now, and his legs steadier, but it was all he could do to keep up. When he stumbled or lagged a stride behind, he felt the cold nose of a gun in the small of his back.

They moved in single file and in complete silence. Not even a twig snapped as they stole through the forest. The leader must have been following a secret trail, known only to the Indians, for they seemed to proceed almost in a straight line. Boughs brushed Dave's face at times but there were no fallen trees or thick undergrowth to slow their passage.

In the dark he had to keep close to the man in front of him to stay in line. He could not see the young brave ahead, but he could hear and smell him. That sickish-sweet odor of sweat and rancid bear's grease was almost overpowering at first. Dave got used to it after a while, but he would never learn to like it.

The swift, steady pace must have covered four or five miles in the first hour. The white boy was too tired to keep track of time or distance. All he could do was hang on doggedly, knowing that if he faltered his chance of life would be slim indeed.

After what seemed an endless time the leader brought them to a halt. They were on the bank of a small, fast-flowing stream. The Indians squatted on the ground and Dave, panting with weariness, was allowed to sit down on a moss-covered log.

They appeared to be waiting for something. There was a whispered consultation and one of the party proceeded to build a tiny fire between two rocks. Greedily the Indians cut off strips of the fresh-killed meat, speared it on green sticks and held it in the flames. As soon as it was scorched on the outside they wolfed it down like animals. Dave was hungry enough to envy them, but no food was offered him. One or the other of his two captors kept a constant watch over him. Even if he had had the strength to make a try, he knew there was no chance of his escaping.

The band stayed there for the better part of an hour. Then, suddenly, silently, other Indians came out on the river bank. There were nine or ten of them, all wearing the same hideous black and white paint pattern as the party that had taken Dave prisoner. With them were more captives. One was a white woman, carrying a tiny baby. Another was a heavy-set, sour-faced boy of about his own age. And the third was a girl, perhaps eleven or twelve years old.

They, too, must have been hurried fast along the trail, for all three were staggering with weariness.

The newly arrived warriors crowded around the fire and grabbed pieces of half-raw meat from the younger braves who were cooking it. Two of them pushed the woman prisoner toward the log where Dave was sitting and he stood up to make room for her. Her face was a pale, set mask and her eyes stared straight ahead. One of the Indians pointed impatiently at the baby and opened the neck of her dress with a rough hand. Moving as if in a dream she put the infant's small, round head against her breast and nursed it.

After perhaps ten minutes another Indian came out of the woods. Sweat gleamed on his back and arms in the starlight, and he was breathing deep, as if he had run a long distance. The braves gathered around him while he panted out a few words. Then they hastily rounded up the prisoners, covered the fire with earth and leaves and took the trail again. Dave felt a surge of hope. He was sure the scout had reported that they were being followed.

For two hours the band pushed down the twisting river bank at a killing pace. Then the leaders swung the column suddenly into the shallow water, waded downstream a hundred yards or more and crossed over to the other side. Two or three warriors stayed behind to wipe out their traces as the party moved through the woods to higher ground.

Somewhere up ahead in the line the white woman stumbled and her child whimpered briefly. There came a low-voiced, threatening snarl from her Indian guard and they went on in silence again.

Dave was so nearly exhausted that he could only plod forward, trying to keep his legs under him. Any hope he had of being rescued was fading now. If a group of white men had started after them, the speed of their march and the well-hidden trail must have left the pursuers far behind.

They crossed two ranges of forest-clad hills and came down a long, rough slope, through heavy timber. It was nearing dawn. The boy could begin to see the tired figures ahead of him as blacker shadows against the dark.

Suddenly the baby began to cry again, its wail sounding startlingly loud in the stillness. The nearest Indian snatched the child from its mother's arms. Dave turned his eyes away quickly but he could not shut his ears. He heard a small, sickening thud and then the savage tossed something away into the brush.

The woman did not scream. Her head bowed lower and she sagged slowly to the ground. Two Indians hauled her to her feet and shook her roughly, but her body hung limp in their hands. By the mercy of Providence she was unconscious.

Dave felt his stomach turn over. He staggered dizzily and might have fallen if the gun muzzle had not punched him in the back again.

A few whispered words were exchanged between the leader of the band and his warriors. Then they picked up the woman and hurried on for a few hundred yards. There was a dense spruce thicket on the right of the trail. Into it the advance guard went, crawling under the low-growing boughs like snakes. One after another the others followed, dragging their captives with them. When Dave was pulled through the last of the brush he found himself in a little open glade, twenty or thirty feet across, with the spruce growing like a wall on every side. It was the kind of hiding-place that deer choose when they go to cover.

Daylight was close at hand now. Moving like ghosts in the gray dawn, the Indians prowled about their prisoners. One of the pair who had captured Dave motioned to him to sit down and keep quiet. He slumped to the ground, stretching his weary legs and shutting his eyes. Then, close to his shoulder, he heard a whisper. It was the little girl. She had stolen quietly near and was squatting there beside him.

"What happened?" she breathed. "Where's the baby?"

Her eyes were wide and serious. He knew he had to tell her the truth.

"Back there," he whispered, nodding toward the woods. "It cried and they—killed it."

She took the news without flinching and stared at him quietly for several seconds.

"He was such a darling baby," she murmured at last. "Only two weeks old. His mother is Judith Gray. She's a neighbor of ours."

She paused and looked soberly at Dave. "Guess you're not from 'round these parts, are you? My name's Nancy Morrison. What's yours?"

The young Indian who had wanted Dave's scalp heard their whispering and sprang toward them. His tomahawk was in his hand and his teeth were bared in a snarl. There was no question about his meaning. Dave knew that if he opened his mouth the savage would welcome the excuse to brain him.

The boy sat still and met the threat in the Indian's eyes with a steady gaze. He might be bound and helpless, but he wasn't going to let any half-fledged brave know that he was scared.

IV

GRADUALLY it grew lighter, but no sunlight came into the glade. What Dave could see of the sky was gray and overcast. For that, at least, he was grateful. As far as he could tell there was no water for the prisoners, and if the sun had been hot it would have added to their torture.

Already he was both thirsty and hungry. As he watched, two of the Indians wrapped the meat they had brought in green leaves to keep out the flies and hung it in the crotch of a tree. They wouldn't risk a cooking fire while they were in hiding.

The young chief called his braves together and gave orders, partly in low-voiced grunts, partly in sign talk. Dave was beginning to understand some of the expressive gestures that served for words. The leader picked out two warriors and sent them out as scouts. His directions were plain enough, even to the white boy. One was to go southeast, across the ridge of hills, and keep an eye on the back trail. He was to stay out about two hours, as indicated by the angle of the chief's arm, pointing eastward to the sky. The other was sent west. Dave wasn't wholly sure of his errand, but since the leader made motions like wielding a paddle, he thought it might have something to do with a canoe.

When they had departed, the rest of the Indians settled down for what appeared to be a long wait. Four or five of them curled up and went to sleep. Several others squatted close to the prisoners, keeping a watchful guard. The young chief sat with his back against a tree and carefully repainted his face with black and white pigments taken from a small buckskin pouch.

He was a handsome fellow in spite of the ferocious-looking paint stripes. About twenty years old, six feet tall, and lithe as a cat, he had the bearing of a born leader. Dave studied the man's face and found no weakness in it. He saw a firm, thin-lipped mouth, a nose like the beak of a hawk, high cheekbones and opaque eyes that narrowed to slits. The Indian's head was shaved except for a roach of coarse black hair in the middle. Two eagle feathers stood up proudly from this scalplock.

Like the rest of the party, the chief was clad only in a deerskin breechclout and moccasins. His one distinguishing ornament was a necklace of long, white teeth—wolves' teeth.

When he finished repairing his war paint, the tall young leader gave his attention to some odd-looking hanks of hair that hung from a thong about his waist. With horror Dave

40

realized that they were scalps. In spite of his feeling of revulsion, he watched, fascinated, as the Indian combed out the tangled locks with his fingers. The first one was that of an old woman. The hair was long and gray and sparse. It was the other scalp that the chief fondled with special pride, and when Dave saw its color he shuddered. Only one man in the settlements could have owned that fiery red thatch.

"Uncle Jed!" he breathed through clenched teeth.

The boy shut his eyes and fought back the feeling of weakness and misery that swept through him. If he meant to do anything about his uncle's murder he must keep himself alive through this ordeal. Somehow, some time, he must find the strength and the opportunity to get away.

When he looked about him again the two young Indians who had taken him prisoner were untying the hands of the captives. The thick-set white boy was lying on his side, dozing. One of the braves kicked him in the back with the toe of his moccasin and when he sat up poured a small quantity of yellow grain into his open palm. It was parched corn—the regular marching ration of tribes on the warpath.

Dave received his handful and tasted it. The dry, flinty kernels were hard to chew, but once he had cracked them with his teeth the flavor was better than he had expected. A few feet away young Nancy Morrison was solemnly munching, her jaws working like a squirrel's.

"She's got more spunk than I have," he thought, with grudging admiration. "Whatever happens to us, she won't be the one to whimper."

He caught her eye and gave her an approving grin.

Over across from them was the woman prisoner. She had recovered from her faint after a few minutes. Now she sat perfectly quiet, her hands in her lap, her face white and still as a statue's. Her eyes·stared blankly, straight ahead.

The young Indian who had been doling out the corn poured some into her empty hands but she made no move to eat it. After a moment, Dave saw one of the warriors get up and walk over to her. The boy had not given any particular attention to this Indian before, but he had a good opportunity to study him now.

He seemed to be older than any of the others—a heavily muscled man with a cruel face. Dave remembered him now as the leader of the second party of braves, who had joined them by the river in the night. As he stood scowling down at the white woman, Dave noticed a huge scar under his ribs on the left side, and a droop to the left shoulder. Some ancient wound had twisted his body and given his back a permanent crook. Three grisly scalps swung from a thong at his waist.

The Indian growled an order to his captive, then motioned to her to eat, putting a hand to his mouth. When she paid no heed, his arm shot out like a striking snake and he slapped her viciously across the face.

Judith Gray made no outcry. Slowly, like one in a trance, she lifted some grains of corn to her lips and began to chew them. The mark of the Indian's hand was a vivid red welt against the pallor of her cheek.

He still stood over her, making sure that she would eat. When he was satisfied he gave a kind of grunt, turned on his heel and went back to his rest.

Dave thought he hated him more than any living thing he had ever known.

.   .   .   .

Before the boy had finished that handful of corn, his mouth was so dry he could barely swallow the last particles. He could understand why the redskins considered corn an ideal diet for the trail. The labor of eating it soon took away one's appetite.

When his breakfast was done, Dave's wrists were bound behind him once more. After that there was nothing to do but sleep if he could—watch the Indians—and try to forget his parching thirst.

Lying on his side he was able to drowse off in a few short naps, but the discomfort of his numb arms soon woke him. In an effort to keep his mind off his desire for water he concentrated on listening to the low-voiced talk of the warriors. By piecing together the sounds and the gestures he thought he could catch the meaning of an occasional word.

Once he saw the youngster he had fought making signs in his direction. Apparently the youth was bragging about his capture. His boasts were soon cut short by a scornful chuckle from the other Indian who had been present and he subsided in embarrassed silence.

These two were of special interest to the white boy,

partly because they were closest to his own age, partly because they seemed to consider him as their personal property.

The older lad—the one who had spared Dave's scalp—was about seventeen, tall and strongly built. He had a small picture of a bear crudely tattooed on the left side of his breast, and the young prisoner knew enough about Indian customs to recognize it as the symbol of the bear totem. Running through all the Indian nations and crossing tribal lines were those mysterious fraternities—the bear, the turtle, the serpent and others he did not know.

Perhaps because Dave knew he owed him his life, he had a more friendly feeling toward this brave than toward any of the rest. He could not help liking the big lad's ready smile, and admiring the way he bore himself among the other warriors.

The younger Indian was more graceful but slighter in build, less sure of himself. He had a quick, nervous way of speaking and moving. There was no totem mark on his chest but, like several of the others, he wore a small pewter cross on a thong about his neck. A mission Indian, possibly from St. Francis, Dave thought. Being the youngest of the party, he seemed to try extra hard to act like a man. There was something of a swagger in his walk, and he did his best to make his youthful face look stern and haughty.

That was the longest day Dave Foster had ever known. It dragged by monotonously, endlessly. If any white men were following the band they must have lost the trail, for

NANCY EDGED CLOSER TO DAVE IN THE GATHERING GLOOM

the scouts came in at intervals of an hour or two and seemed to have nothing to report.

There was ample time for the white boy to wonder what lay ahead for the prisoners. He had heard horrible tales of torture at the stake. It was quite possible, he thought, that when the Indians were sure of their safety from pursuit, they would hold a war dance and skin and burn their captives. Squirming, he tried not to let his mind dwell on that picture. There was always the other chance—that they might be taken as slaves to the Indian villages in Canada. That, too, was a harsh and dreary prospect. He knew there was a third possibility. The moment might come when he could make a break for freedom or be killed quickly and mercifully in the attempt.

In the afternoon the air grew hot and close in the glade. The sky darkened and rumbles of thunder, starting low and far away, became louder as the storm approached.

Nancy edged closer to Dave in the gathering gloom. He thought for a moment that she was afraid of the thunder, but her smile was serene. She might have been a pretty child under other circumstances. Her yellow hair was tangled now, and there were sticks and leaves in it. Her calico gown was torn by briars and her bare legs showed bloody scratches.

"I hope it rains quick," she whispered. "And hard, too. I'm awful thirsty, aren't you?"

He looked about to make sure the Indians were not listening and breathed an answer. "I sure am," he told her. "But don't talk or they'll beat you."

The girl nodded and looked hopefully up at the threatening sky.

When the first big drops began to fall, the braves stirred themselves and a few crawled into the shelter of the spruce thicket. The rest sat stolidly where they were and let the rain sluice off their well-greased shoulders. Dave tilted his head back, shut his eyes against the downpour and opened his mouth as wide as he could.

It was a heavy, drenching rain. He was grateful for the taste of the hard-driven drops on his dry tongue, but it was surprising how little water seemed to find its way into his mouth. Long before his thirst was really satisfied, the storm rolled off to the northward and the rain ceased.

By the time the clouds were gone the sun was setting. The young chief stood up and stretched his powerful arms. Then he put his hands to his mouth and a startling cry shattered the silence. It was a perfect imitation of a loon's crazy laughter. He did not need to repeat the call. Within five minutes the scouts came hurrying in. The braves took their bundles of meat out of the tree, picked up their weapons and booty, and prodded the prisoners to their feet. While it was still light enough to see in the woods, they took to the trail again.

Dave felt better after his day's rest. Though his stomach seemed to have shrunk to a small, aching knot, he was stronger and less subject to dizzy spells. The effects of the blow on the head must be wearing off.

They moved fast through a belt of hardwood—rock maple,

48

hickory and ash. Then, climbing over a low ridge, they were in the pines again. It was too dark to see the shapes of the trees but Dave could tell by the sound of the wind in the boughs and the slippery feel of the pine needle carpet under his feet.

He thought they had been on the march about two hours when the ground began to go downhill and he heard the soft lap of waves a short distance ahead. A few moments later they came to a halt on the shore of a lake. Under the starlight it stretched westward mile after mile, broken here and there by wooded points and islands. A light breeze stirred its surface and sent waves splashing against the rocky bank.

The chief motioned the captives back into the shadows and set off with two of his warriors to reconnoiter the shoreline to the south. Three other scouts, under the command of the crooked-backed brave, went northward.

The prisoners and their guards sat down to wait. Nancy Morrison wriggled close to Dave's side, laid her tousled head on his knee and went to sleep. He had never felt anything but a lofty masculine contempt for girls before. This one, by her uncomplaining courage, had won his respect. She was as game as any boy, and he felt proud that she trusted him.

A half hour went by. Then a long, dark shadow moved silently up the lake shore. Against the starlit water Dave could see the outline of a big canoe with three men at the paddles. The young chief stepped out of the craft into the shallows and pulled it up on a little shelf of beach. It was

longer and wider than any canoe the boy had seen before—
a war canoe, he guessed.

After a few minutes, two more of the long, slim, birch-
bark boats appeared from the northward. The Indians must
have left them hidden in the brush when they made their
foray against the Contoocook settlements. As the last of the
canoes touched shore, the chief motioned the rest of the
party to him. The prisoners were roused and hustled down
to the beach. The meat, the stolen kettles and finery were
loaded aboard. Dave found Nancy and himself pushed into
the middle of the chief's canoe, where they sat in the bottom,
surrounded by neatly stowed piles of duffel. Six Indians
shoved the craft into deeper water and climbed in, laying
their guns beside them. Then each took up a spruce paddle.
There was no word of command. The six blades dipped in
perfect unison and the canoe shot forward silently, keeping
close to the shadow of the woods.

V

THEY had traveled only a few hundred yards when Dave caught the muffled sound of a distant musket shot. It came from somewhere to the east, beyond the last range of hills they had crossed.

The young chief was in the bow. He held up his hand and the paddles stopped in mid-air. Then he rose to his feet, listening. In a moment the report of a gun came again, this time, Dave thought, from farther to the south. Excitement made his heart beat faster. If he interpreted the sounds correctly, there were white men on their track. One party must have picked up the trail and signaled to another group. The second shot would be their answer.

The Indian leader yelped some kind of an order in Abenaki and the other two canoes pushed off hastily. Dave saw them come tearing through the water, paddles flying, and the chief's canoe was also in motion again. The white boy had never known that anything afloat could go so fast.

He felt the wind whip his hair, and as he watched the shore-line flow past he knew they were traveling at a pace few men could match on foot.

The lake stretched some seven or eight miles to the westward, and the three canoes covered that distance in a little more than an hour of furious paddling. As they neared the pine-clad shore at the farther end, the paddles moved more slowly and the chief knelt in the bow, his eyes searching the darkness ahead. They rounded a low, marshy point where the water was so shallow the blades scraped bottom at each stroke. Then Dave saw they were in a narrow channel, flanked by reeds. There was a perceptible current carrying the canoe along. They were in a stream which must be the outlet of the lake.

Gradually the banks grew higher and the current ran faster. Looking astern, Dave could see the other canoes moving, ghostly, in their wake. His eyelids grew heavy and after a few minutes he curled up as best he could and went to sleep.

He was roused, some time later, by the grating of the bark bottom on gravel. The canoe lay close to the bank and the Indians were taking out their guns and belongings. Dave stood up, still groggy with sleep. As soon as he and Nancy had been hustled ashore, he was surprised to find that his hands had been untied.

One of the young savages grunted a couple of words in Abenaki and pointed at a pile of duffel on the ground. Obediently Dave picked up as much as he could carry. Four of the Indians hoisted the big canoe to their shoulders and set off along the rough trail that bordered the stream. Prodded from behind, the boy joined the procession and went stumbling over the rocks in the darkness.

When they had gone a hundred yards he saw the reason for the carry. Below, on his left, the river went plunging over a ten-foot fall into a gorge. They made a circuit of nearly half a mile before it was possible to launch the canoes again.

There was a level spot at the end of the portage, where the chief halted the party for a few minutes to eat and rest. Apparently they had stored some food with the canoes, for in addition to the parched corn Dave was given a small strip of tough, dry meat—moose meat, he thought. It was almost as hard to chew as the corn but it had a pleasant, smoky taste and he was hungry enough to enjoy it.

This time there was no lack of water to wash down the dry meal. The river ran clear and cool at their feet and the prisoners were allowed to drink all they wanted.

When the canoes were put in the water Dave expected his wrists would be bound once more. Instead, the bigger of the two young braves who had captured him thrust a paddle into his hands and motioned for him to kneel by the gunwale. The boy was taken by surprise, but he made up his mind that he wouldn't give them anything to laugh at.

He had grown up close to the Cocheco, the Piscataqua and Great Bay, and had been in and out of canoes ever since he could remember. Paddling this larger craft was different, but he watched the man ahead of him as well as he could in the dark, and tried to imitate his stroke and timing. Apparently he was doing better than they expected, for there was no mirth in the muttered comments of the two young braves.

In some ways the steady work of paddling was better than sitting still. It took his mind off his troubles. Instead of feeling sorry for himself he concentrated on perfecting the short, quick Indian stroke and the silent flip of the blade that left no splash.

After an hour or two the muscles in his back and shoulders began to ache, but soon the water grew swifter and the canoes were beached for another carry. Dave stood up and stretched. The young Indian with the bear tattoo was just behind him. The white boy felt a hand pat his back in approval, and when he turned he caught the flash of the young brave's teeth in a grin.

As before, he carried a load of duffel across the portage. This one was longer—close to a mile, he judged—but the savages carrying the big craft never stopped to rest. They went at a dogtrot, up hill and down, till they reached the bank of the river once more.

When they climbed into the canoe, Dave reached for the paddle, but this time he was pushed down into his old place in the bottom. The reason was soon apparent. He felt the current pick up speed and in a moment they were in a long stretch of white water, shooting down through a maze of rocks and tossing spray. He could do well enough in smooth

HE CONCENTRATED ON PERFECTING THE SHORT, QUICK
INDIAN STROKE

water but this kind of canoemanship was beyond his skill.

Dave held his breath, exhilarated by the wild ride. Nancy had been wakened to make the portage and now she sat beside him, her eyes wide but unterrified.

"Can you swim?" he heard her whisper.

He nodded.

"So can I," she said. "But I don't think we're going to tip over. This is fun! You didn't tell me your name so I don't know what to call you."

"David," he told her. "David Foster."

The roar of the rapids drowned out the sound of their whispers and the Indians were too busy to pay any attention to them. Nancy had to speak close to his ear to make herself heard.

"Where do you think they're taking us, David?" she asked.

"I don't know. Canada, most likely. Look—what about your folks? What happened to them?"

She shivered a little. "I wish I knew," she said. "Daddy and Mother and my little brother were in the house when they came. They caught me down in the meadow where I'd gone to get the cow. There was a lot of shooting after that and I saw one Indian get killed. They burned the cowshed but maybe they didn't get into the house."

The canoe tilted dangerously as it scraped a rock, then righted itself and shot out into smoother water below the rapids. There was no more chance for the young captives to talk.

The night was beginning to fade into dawn when they passed a clearing by the river. The canoes drifted past it in silence, keeping close under the shadow of woods on the opposite bank. In the dim light Dave made out the black shape of a fire-gutted cabin, back in the clearing. In the canoe close astern he saw the crooked-backed warrior point toward the burned house and wave a scalp in the air with a gesture of triumph. The boy knew then that the band had been this way before.

Two or three miles downstream the leader motioned the canoes ashore. Dave thought it was another carry until he saw the warriors slide the three craft into a jack-pine thicket. They went up into the woods a short distance and burrowed through dense undergrowth to enter a hiding place much like the one where they had holed up the day before.

There was one difference, this time, and an important one. At the far side of the open glade Dave saw a spring, with a trickle of clear water flowing out of it. One after another of the warriors knelt and drank. Then the prisoners were given their chance. After a breakfast of parched corn, Dave and the other boy had their wrists bound behind them once more. The two female captives were allowed the use of their hands.

Judith Gray still sat apart, her face white and expressionless. After a while Nancy went over to her side. The girl tried to comfort her as best she could, but was met by stony silence. Dave wondered whether the woman's mind was gone.

That day seemed to pass more swiftly, perhaps because the boy was getting adjusted to his new way of living. He found that sleep came more easily, and when he woke up, late in the afternoon, he felt well rested.

Another handful of corn was passed around when sunset came and this time dried moose meat was added to the meal. They went back to the canoes in the dusk. To Dave's satisfaction he was allowed to handle a paddle on most of the night's journey. Two or three hours before dawn there was a long, downhill carry to avoid a series of falls. When they returned to the bank at the lower end of the portage, the boy saw a broad valley opening ahead of them. The stream down which they had been paddling joined a much larger river just ahead. Dave knew where they were now. They had reached the valley of the Connecticut.

.   .   .   .

The Indians held a brief council before launching their birch-bark craft. It was too dark for Dave to gather much from their gestures, but the question seemed to be whether they should push on into the big river or wait for the cover of the next night.

It was quickly settled. They repacked the canoes and shoved off, paddling hard. There was still half a mile or more of the smaller stream to negotiate before they entered the Connecticut. After a few minutes the chief motioned them into the overhanging alders along the shore. He grunted half a dozen words of command and two of the braves crawled over the cargo to Dave's side. He felt his wrists being tied behind him. Then a wad of dirty deerskin was crammed into his mouth and tied in place with a raw-hide thong. He tried angrily to voice his objections but could make only a muffled, choking sound. The savages gagged Nancy in the same way, then returned to their places. The flotilla moved on, stealing along under the shadows of the bank in complete silence. They rounded a low point and swung to the right, bucking the current of the broad river and staying close to its eastern shore.

Looking out across the black water, Dave could see the reason for their precautions. On the farther bank, a quarter of a mile away, were the dark shapes of houses—three or four of them. And in the largest one a tiny flicker of candlelight shone through a window. Unless he was mistaken, the structure from which the light came was a blockhouse, built with an overhang to repel attacks. The fact that the savages were so careful to avoid it must mean that it was a fairly strong settlement, with a garrison of soldiers.

They had made several hundred yards upstream when a dog began barking inside the settlement's stockade. There was no sound of a command, but the big canoe shot ahead with increased speed. The paddlers bent their backs to it, driving with all their might. Quickly the houses dropped astern and the dog's excited warning grew fainter in the distance. After four or five minutes the flotilla rounded a bend in the river and the tension among the Indians relaxed. In answer to a guttural remark by the chief, the young braves chuckled and slowed their stroke. Through the slowly graying light of dawn Dave saw the shapes of the other canoes close behind.

A full hour had passed and they must have covered four or five miles before the gags were taken from the prisoners' mouths.

It was broad daylight now. The chief motioned with his arm and all three craft pulled into a sheltered cove on the eastern bank. There the duffel was unloaded and the canoes concealed in a thicket. A short distance up the wooded slope there was dense spruce cover where the party went into hiding.

All morning Dave pretended to sleep. Actually he was wide awake, his senses on the alert. There was a chance, he thought, that someone in the garrison might have seen the canoes as they passed. In these outposts on the frontier there were sometimes experienced trackers and fighting men— members of Rogers' famous Rangers, perhaps. If they had taken up the chase at dawn, there was a real possibility of rescue.

As the hours passed and nothing happened, the boy's hopes sagged. A little before noon he saw the crooked-backed warrior and another brave pick up their guns and steal off through the woods. The young chief scowled after them as if he didn't approve of whatever they meant to do, but he made no move to stop them.

Two hours later Dave was wakened from a doze by the sound of distant shots. There was sudden activity among the Indians. All the braves snatched up their guns and stood listening. At a muttered order from the leader, three of them hurried away in different directions. Those who were left loosened the hatchets at their belts, looked to the priming of their muskets and kept a constant watch, their beady eyes staring into the forest.

Dave did not dare to speak, but he glanced at Nancy and tried to encourage her with a smile. The other white boy, whose name, he had learned, was Joshua Boles, looked fidgety and scared. His heavy face was pale as he watched the Indians' preparations for trouble. Among the four captives, only Judith Gray seemed unaware of what was happening. As always she sat quiet with that blank look of horror in her eyes.

The minutes dragged by and Dave felt the tension mount. His throat felt tight and dry as he watched the motionless figures of the crouching redskins. After a long time he heard the chatter of a squirrel close at hand. There was no other sound, but the eyes of the Indians were all turned in one direction.

Then he saw it—a single dark figure moving quickly toward them among the spruces. It was the brave with the cruel mouth and the twisted back. His chest was heaving and sweat ran down his painted face. His musket was gone, but in his hand he held up a red and dripping scalp. There was blood on the blade of his tomahawk.

In answer to a curt question from the chief, he gasped out a few words and pointed southward down the river. The young leader frowned, lifted his head and gave the loon call.

Within half a minute the three scouts had come in and the party was hurrying down the hill to the canoes.

That was the quickest loading and launching Dave had ever seen. Almost before he knew it he was in the lead canoe with the paddle in his hands. He stole one look down the river, but there was no sign of a pursuing boat. Then the light craft darted ahead and he was wielding the blade mechanically, in time with the other paddlers.

VI

IT WAS a sultry afternoon. The sun blazed down on the water and Dave felt the sweat start before he had taken twenty strokes. The pace the Indians set was a killing one. They were paddling for their lives. He kept up as best he could till an ache came between his shoulder blades and the panting breath caught in his throat. Once he slumped forward, trying to rest for a few strokes, but the sharp tip of a paddle was thrust into his ribs and he jerked up again. Angry that they should think him a weakling, he dug in harder than ever.

After a while he seemed to get his second wind. His arms moved steadily, almost without feeling. He knew the canoes must have come a long way but his mind was too tired to think about it. Nancy's voice close to his ear started his brain working again.

"I guess they aren't coming after us," the girl murmured.

"No," he answered in a frog-like croak. "We got away."

Something about that struck him as funny. He began to laugh and couldn't stop. The paddle slipped out of his hands and fell in the bottom of the canoe, but this time he wasn't prodded back to work. Only the steersman at the stern was paddling now. The light craft glided in toward the shore and came to a stop under overhanging trees.

The Indians didn't bother to unload. They tied the canoes there and crawled up on the bank, where they flung themselves on the ground to rest. The boy knew then that they were as tired as he was. Only one of them—the chief—crouched with his back against a tree and kept watch.

Sprawled there in the cool shade Dave fell asleep almost at once. When he woke, someone was shaking his shoulder. He struggled up to a sitting posture and found the young brave with the bear tattooed on his chest grinning down at him. The Indian pointed to his mouth and gave him a handful of corn and a sliver of smoked meat.

When he tried to eat he found he had very little appetite. His stomach felt shriveled and small, and his belt, pulled to the last notch, was loose around his middle. Nevertheless, chewing on the dry corn brought the saliva back into his mouth, and his desire for food returned after the first swallow. By the time he had finished his ration and drunk deep of the clear river water, the Indians were gathering beside the canoes once more.

The sun was low in the west when they resumed their journey. A short distance up the river they came to a narrow place between high rocks and saw rapids ahead. They made a portage of a mile or more. When the canoes were put into the water again, the paddling was more leisurely.

After darkness came, the Indian behind Dave motioned to him to lie down on the duffel and get some rest. The boy was glad to obey. He was dog-tired after the effort of the afternoon. At intervals through the night he woke to find the canoe still moving steadily upstream. Between darkness and dawn, the party must have put another fifteen miles of river behind them.

When they went ashore at daylight the prisoners were bound once more. Though Dave did not know it then, it was the last time he was to feel those chafing thongs on his wrists. The weary Indians slept wherever they happened to drop. A single guard—the scarred and twisted warrior whose scalping foray had so nearly brought trouble to the band the day before—remained awake and watchful.

Dave wasn't sleepy. He sat on the root of a big pine tree, his back against the trunk, and took stock of his situation. He had heard of prisoners who had escaped from the Indians when their captors got drunk. But there was no firewater in this party. Apparently all the cabins they had raided had belonged to teetotalers. As long as they stayed sober he knew there was only the barest chance of his getting away un-observed. And now, to complicate matters, he had young Nancy to consider. Making a break for himself and leaving her behind was unthinkable.

He was no longer afraid of starving to death, for the slim diet of parched corn and moose meat seemed to be agreeing

66

with him. Thin as he had grown, he felt strong enough, and his endurance was good. His shirt and breeches hung in tatters about him, but the moose-hide moccasins were still serviceable. Barring accidents he was pretty sure he could stand the journey to Canada.

By noonday the war party was awake and stirring. They ate again, then loaded the canoes and made a start.

The paddling that afternoon was done at an even, steady stroke that ate up the distance. When dusk began to fall, Dave figured they were at least forty miles above the last white settlement.

The lead canoe was stealing along in the shadows, close to shore, when the young chief suddenly held up his hand in warning. A hundred yards ahead, in the shallow water below the bank, Dave saw a cow moose. She was munching on the succulent stems of pond lilies, her head completely under water except for the great ears that flicked forward and back, twitching off the flies.

The Indians feathered the blades of their paddles, moving them forward through the water to prevent any sound of splashing. The boy used the same silent stroke, and the canoe slipped nearer yard by yard. Up in the bow the chief reached behind him and picked up his musket. He looked at the priming, shook his head and put the gun back without a sound. Instead, he took a heavy cedar bow from the bottom of the canoe. Bending it, he slipped the loop of the deer-sinew cord over the notched end, drew a feathered arrow from the quiver and fitted it to the string.

They had covered more than half the distance to the feeding moose before her sensitive ears warned her of danger. Her head came up with a spatter of drops and her startled eyes looked full at them. In that second, before she could move, the chief's bow twanged and the arrow flew straight to its mark. It plunged home in the cow's side, low and behind the shoulder.

She gave one convulsive bound that carried her halfway up the bank. Then she collapsed, sliding slowly back into the mud. With a yell of triumph the Indians drove their paddles deep, and in another moment the canoe was alongside the dead moose. The other two craft were close behind. Jumping into the water, the braves laid hold of the huge animal and dragged the carcass up to dry land. When the chief pulled out his arrow, half the length of the shaft was crimson with blood. It had been a perfect shot, right through the heart.

Chattering gaily at the prospect of a feast, the Indians went to work with their skinning knives. In almost no time they had whipped off the hide and were cutting up the still warm meat. At a nod from the chief, some of the younger warriors built a small cooking fire in the angle of a ledge. They seemed to feel they were far enough ahead of any pursuers to forget their usual precautions.

There was fresh roast meat for everybody that night. Dave found it tough-fibered and strong to the taste, but as a change from the diet of the past few days it was welcome enough. After a few mouthfuls he was satisfied. He didn't

THE CHIEF'S BOW TWANGED AND THE ARROW FLEW STRAIGHT
TO THE MARK

seem to have as much room for food in his stomach as formerly.

The Indians, however, had no such difficulty. Slobbering like dogs over the smoking chunks of meat, they gorged themselves till they could hardly stagger.

Watching them, the boy began to wonder if he could smuggle Nancy away after the camp had gone to sleep. He was sure they could outrun any of the braves after that meal. But his hopes soon died. The chief ordered the fire put out and the prisoners taken back to the canoes. In a few minutes they were on their way again.

The Indians grunted and puffed over their paddling but the food had put them in a good humor. No longer afraid to make a noise, they joked among themselves and belched loudly and cheerfully.

Some time around midnight they reached a spot they seemed to know. It was a pine-clad point where the river made a bend at the head of a long reach. There they beached the canoes on firm sand. The remaining moose meat was hung high in the boughs of a tree, a pair of braves took over sentinel duty, and the rest of the party lay down to sleep.

It was a calm, starry night, but there was a chill in the air. Dave scooped handfuls of the dry pine needles into a sort of nest and made himself as comfortable as he could. Toward morning he dreamed of being cold, and thinking he was in his bed at home he reached down to pull up the blanket. All his groping hand discovered was his own torn breeches and bare ankles. Shivering, he drew his knees as high as he could and huddled there, half asleep, till daybreak.

Even the Indians felt the frosty sharpness before dawn. They got up one by one, shaking themselves like animals. By sunrise they had eaten a sketchy breakfast and were back in the canoes.

That afternoon they passed the mouth of a fairly large river flowing in from the northwest. The young Indian with the bear totem pointed to it with his paddle. "Passumpsic," he said, and repeated the word for Dave's benefit. When the boy made a try at pronouncing it, the young brave seemed pleased.

He aimed a finger toward his own breast.

"Nequanis," he said, slowly and distinctly.

"Nequanis," Dave echoed, and the Indian lad grinned and nodded.

Next he pointed to the other young brave who had shared in Dave's capture. "Matawassie," he said, and again the white boy repeated the name.

Nothing would do then but for Dave to tell them his own name, and they mastered it after a try or two.

"Da-vit," they pronounced it over and over, delighted with their success.

During the rest of that day the boy learned a score of words in Abenaki while they paddled on up the river. Nancy, sitting at his side, picked up the queer-sounding words as quickly as he did, and the two Indians were obviously proud of their pupils. The chief made no comment but let them jabber as much as they liked.

The channel of the Connecticut was narrower now, and there were shallows, where the canoes had to pick their way among rocks. Twice, before dark, they made short carries around white water.

It was cold again that night, but Dave prepared for it by pulling armfuls of fir tips for Nancy and himself. The Indians scorned such luxuries. They curled up, half naked as they were, while the young white prisoners burrowed into their heaps of evergreen.

Dave heard the girl yawn in the darkness. "Thank you, David," she murmured. "I 'most froze to death last night, but I'm comf'table now."

The flotilla passed the mouth of the Amonoosuc late the following day. At dusk, as they were coming in to make a landing, one of the braves in the second canoe spotted a deer swimming across the river. All three craft swung about instantly in pursuit, and they overtook the frightened animal in midstream. With a whoop, the Indian who had first sighted it dove into the water. He seized the buck by one of its antlers and plunged his hunting knife deep into its throat. When the poor beast's struggles were over they hauled it to shore and prepared for another feast.

As soon as a fire could be built the choicest parts of the meat were cut up and handed around. Dave found himself holding a long green stick with a piece of venison as big as his fist impaled on the end. He held it in the hot flames for several minutes, turning it steadily. Most of the Indians barely seared the outside of the meat before biting into it. Even though he was among the last to start eating, the boy found the inside of his chunk nearly raw. He went back to the fire several times before he finished.

At daybreak next morning they were on the way again. There was a zest about their paddling and an eagerness in the young braves' skylarking that came from something more than well-filled stomachs. Dave was beginning to understand scraps of their conversation but he was still puzzled. At last Nequanis let out a high-pitched yell and pointed ahead.

"Co-hos!" he cried. "Co-hos!" And the other Indians picked up the word in a joyful chant.

Looking up the river, Dave saw the wooded bluffs fall away to left and right. Instead of the dark forest a broad stretch of meadowland spread out on either bank. It was as lovely an intervale as he had ever seen.

The paddlers increased the speed of the stroke and he was hard put to keep up with them. After ten or fifteen minutes he discovered the reason for their zeal. In the lee of a clump of pines near the shore he saw a solid-looking log hut, flanked by several bark wigwams. Running toward the bank was an Indian boy of ten or twelve.

The youngster yelled and waved his arms. In a moment he was joined by a score of other redskins. Most of them were squaws, but Dave saw a few old men and children among them. As the canoes drove in toward shore the braves in the war party shouted greetings and held up the scalps they had taken, bragging of their prowess.

Five minutes later the canoes had been unloaded and the Indians were parading their prisoners before the camp. The stares and giggles of the young squaws gave Dave an uncomfortable feeling. They were a stocky, unattractive lot, for the most part. They were dressed in dirty deerskin leggins and shirts, their coarse black hair hanging in braids down their backs.

After half an hour the chief, whose name, Dave had learned, was Cochequa, stopped their gabble with a lifted hand. He shooed the squaws back to their work in the fields and led the way toward the log shack. There was an old woman sitting in the sun outside the low doorway.

Cochequa spoke to her, motioning first toward the building, then toward the little group of prisoners. She got up, pulled aside the moosehide that covered the door, and hobbled inside. When she returned she was carrying an armful of ragged old blankets. One of them was passed to each of the captives—the two boys first, then Judith Gray and Nancy.

Dave fingered his blanket and tried to look pleased. It was a piece of shoddy trade goods of the kind the French exchanged for beaver and mink skins. He thought it must have been used for years without washing, for it was threadbare, stiff with dirt and redolent of rancid bear's grease.

Nancy stole a glance at him and made a little face, but she was careful not to let the chief see her disgust.

"I guess we're s'posed to be thankful," she told him under her breath.

"Yes," he said, "and maybe we will be if the nights keep getting colder. I sure hope we get a chance to wash 'em, though!"

VII

WHILE the women toiled with their crude wooden hoes among the corn, the older braves in the war party squatted in a ring and held a council. Dave watched them from a respectful distance. There was no talk at first. The chief filled a stone pipe, lighted it with a coal from the fire and took several slow puffs. Then he passed it to the warrior sitting next to him and so it went around the circle.

Nequanis and Matawassie were not included in the council because of their age. When Dave saw them taking fish-lines and hooks from their woodchuck-skin pouches, he asked if he could go with them. Nequanis gave him a nod and a grin and the three youths set off for the river.

There was a well-trodden path leading down the steep bank. At its foot a big, flat-topped rock thrust out into the water, and Dave hurried to it joyfully. While the fishermen moved off upstream, he began scrubbing his blanket with water and clean sand.

In fifteen minutes of hard work he succeeded in removing all the dirt and most of the smell. Then he spread the blanket out in the sun to dry and went to find Nancy. She was sitting beside Judith Gray, chattering like a magpie as she tried to cheer her up. In the past day or two the older woman had seemed more normal. She no longer stared vacantly into space as if in a trance. Yet there were lines of such terrible sadness in her face that Dave could hardly bear to look at her.

"Hi, Nance," he said to the girl. "Come on, I've found a place to wash your blanket. Bring Mrs. Gray's along, too. This sun'll dry 'em before dark."

They went down to the rock and set to work. A few hundred yards up the river they could see Matawassie wading in the shallows. His alder-sapling rod was bent almost in a half circle as he braced his body to hold whatever it was that fought at the other end of the line.

After a brief struggle the Indian boy heaved a huge trout out of the water. They could see the spray flying and hear his triumphant yell as the fish landed flopping on the bank. The river must have been full of trout, for it was only a moment before Nequanis, too, brought a big one ashore. Dave and Nancy hurried through their washing. They were eager to go upstream and get a closer view of the fishing.

There were seven trout lying in the grass when they reached the spot. The biggest fish ran up to three or four pounds in weight and none was under a foot long.

IT TOOK ALL THE BOY'S STRENGTH TO HOLD THE ARCHING ROD
AGAINST THE RUSHES OF THE FIGHTING TROUT

Nequanis looked up and saw Dave and Nancy standing on the bank. With a generous gesture he beckoned to the boy to take his pole, and in sign language he indicated Dave was to catch a grasshopper for bait. That took only a matter of seconds, for there were plenty of the long-legged insects in the tall meadow grass of the intervale. He sprang down to the water's edge and thrust the grasshopper on the hook. Kicking off his moccasins, he waded confidently out into the current.

Somewhat to his surprise, he fished for five minutes without getting so much as a nibble. Matawassie meanwhile had hauled out two more fish and was laughing at him.

"Here," he said to Nequanis, "there must be a trick to this. You take it."

Chuckling, the young Indian flicked the pole back and cast upstream to a still spot just above a ripple. He gave the bait a light jerk or two, so that the grasshopper seemed to be kicking along the surface. And almost instantly a big trout struck at the lure.

Nequanis gave the pole a quick tug to set the hook and handed it back to Dave with a laugh. The tackle was too heavy to break, but it took all the boy's strength to hold the arching rod against the rushes of the fighting trout.

Twice he wrestled it into shoal water only to find the taut line dragging him out again. At last he got a good foothold, lifted the fish clear and flung it high on the bank behind him. When he took it off the hook and measured its length against the others he was proud to find it bigger than any of them.

Dave tried his luck again, imitating Nequanis' methods, and this time he hooked and landed a fish that was all his own. After that he spent his time catching grasshoppers for the two Indians. By the time that afternoon was over they had more than thirty huge trout strung by the gills on alder shoots.

Their return was greeted by shouts of pleasure from the braves, whose council was just breaking up. The squaws came in from the fields and immediately started preparations for a feast. As soon as fires had been built, the fish were gutted and wrapped in damp clay from the riverbank. Then armfuls of green corn were brought in. When the first flames had died down and beds of coals were glowing red, the fish and the ears of corn, still in the husk, were shoved into the embers to roast. In a few minutes everyone was eating lustily.

Dave and Nancy shared a trout between them, and each had two ears of corn. The food was a wonderful change from the hard rations they had eaten on most of the journey. The scaly skin of the fish came off with the clay shell, leaving firm, pink meat beneath, and the corn, though small and nubbly to look at, was tender and almost sweet.

When Dave had eaten all he wanted, he looked around for Josh Boles. Up to now he had found no opportunity to talk to the other boy. Josh was gnawing at an ear of corn and there were four or five corncobs around his feet.

"Hi," said Dave. "It's time we got acquainted. I'm Dave

Foster, from Dover. How are you getting along?"

Josh eyed him suspiciously, almost as if he thought Dave had designs on his food. He grunted some sort of answer and Dave came closer.

"I'm waiting for a chance to get away," he whispered. "Are you game to try?"

Josh had a scared look and he nearly choked on a mouthful of corn. "Naw," he muttered. "It's too far now. They'd ketch us an' skin us alive. This ain't so bad, if we git enough to eat. All you'll do is start trouble. Besides, I've got folks that'll ransom me back."

He thrust a grubby hand inside his shirt and pulled out still another ear of corn which he proceeded to eat. Dave watched him a minute, then turned away, disgusted.

The prisoners were ordered to sleep in one of the bark wigwams that night. The air was close and smelly, and Dave would have preferred rolling up in his dry blanket out-of-doors. However, he was given no choice, and after a restless half hour he slept soundly till morning.

Everybody was up and stirring at dawn. The council, Dave discovered, had decided to leave a detachment of warriors to hunt and guard the work camp in the intervale.

Cochequa commanded one of the remaining canoes, and Bemokis, the Indian with the twisted body, captained the other. As before, Dave and Nancy rode in the young chief's craft, along with Nequanis, Matawassie and three other braves.

They made nearly thirty miles that day. The river grew

narrower and shallower as they advanced, and there were frequent carries.

"Soon," Nequanis told the white boy, in a mixture of sign talk and Abenaki, "we leave canoes, go on foot."

Each day of their journey Dave was learning more words in the Indian tongue. When the young braves talked among themselves he could understand the drift of most that was said. And the language no longer sounded harsh and guttural to him. He even found a kind of music in some of the phrases they used.

At night, when they camped on the bluffs along the stream, there was a sharp warning of coming autumn in the air. As nearly as Dave could figure, it was now well along in August, and they had traveled so far north that frost might be expected any time. He was glad of such warmth as the old blanket gave him.

Three days after they left the Co-hos intervales, they were in rough, rocky country where the river seemed to be hardly more than a brook. At noon they reached a long pond below a waterfall and paddled in toward the left bank. There, in a grove of spruce, Dave saw a row of canoe racks where half a dozen birch canoes were turned bottom up.

Methodically the Indians unloaded all the duffel, tied the paddles under the thwarts, and laid the two canoes on the racks. Then they set about making packs of their loot and supplies. Each of the warriors carried about forty pounds, and Dave and Josh Boles were loaded with similar packs. Even Nancy was given a small one to carry.

Some of the Indians used tumplines over their foreheads to support the load. Dave's pack, wrapped securely in his blanket, was fitted with shoulder straps of rawhide. It rode comfortably on his back and he felt, at the start, as if he could carry it all day.

There were big, rugged-looking hills on their right as they took the trail northeastward. From what little he knew of the geography of the country, Dave thought they must be part of the rocky barrier known as the Height of Land— the mountain ridge that divided the colonies from Canada. If he was right, that meant the party was already out of the Hampshire Grants and in French territory.

They followed an easy, well-beaten path for two hours or more. Then they branched off to the right on a much narrower trail, marked only by faint blazes. Dave pointed to the main path they had left and asked Nequanis where it led.

"St. Francis," the young Indian told him.

"But," said Dave, surprised, "aren't you from St. Francis?"

Nequanis shook his head and wrinkled his nose in disdain. "No," he replied. "The St. Francis tribes are Penacooks and Assagunticooks. We are of the Kennebecs and Penobscots. Our place is many suns away." He waved his arm toward the northeast. "We go to that place now. It is called by the French 'Rivière des Loups'—River of the Wolves."

It was the first time Dave had heard that name, and at the sound of it a chill of foreboding ran up his spine. He thought of it again that night at dusk, when he stumbled, bone-tired, into a sheltered glade where they were to camp. The Indians at the head of the straggling line had already thrown off their packs and were gathering wood for a fire. At that moment there came through the forest a far-off, mournful howl that raised the short hairs at the back of the boy's neck.

"Wolf," said Nequanis unconcernedly. "There are many in these woods, but we have nothing to fear. They will keep away from the fire."

No howling of wolves could have kept Dave awake that night. His pack had grown heavier, mile by mile, and all the muscles in his body ached with weariness. For their evening meal they ate the last of the fresh meat. When the boy had swallowed his portion he tumbled into his blanket and was asleep in an instant.

The Indians were afoot again before daylight. Dave was stiff when he got up, but by the time he had his pack strapped on, he felt better. They did not stop to build a breakfast fire. Each brave and each prisoner took a handful of parched corn to munch on as they went, and without further delay they started up the trail.

Nancy Morrison was having a struggle as she tried to get her small pack settled on her back. Dave helped her adjust the shoulder straps.

"How are you making out?" he asked. "Feel pretty tired after yesterday?"

She laughed. "Not me," she told him with a toss of her head. "My Mom used to say I was a tomboy, so I guess I can keep up."

There must have been a whalebone toughness in the girl, he thought. She was very thin, and her brown arms and legs were covered with scratches, but her spirits were still high.

Dave glanced around at the other two prisoners. Josh Boles looked dejected as he slouched along under his pack. Judith Gray had grown gaunter day by day, but her face was as expressionless as ever. She had little to carry besides her blanket, and once started she kept pace with the other marchers.

They did not hurry but they went steadily, hour after hour. Dave watched Matawassie, who was just ahead of him. He found there was a trick to walking with a pack. The Indian leaned forward from the hips and took long strides, his knees bent a little, his weight falling on the balls of his feet rather than on the heels. The white boy tried it and found he grew tired much less quickly.

Through that day and the monotonous days that followed, Dave made rapid progress in learning the Abenaki language. Nequanis and Matawassie had plenty of breath for talk and storytelling. When they found that Dave was beginning to understand them, they were delighted, and from that time on they took turns in recounting the old legends of their people.

Dave heard tales of the mighty deeds performed by bygone chiefs of the Penobscots and Kennebecs. He heard, too, of the kind-hearted giant Glooskap and his battles with the wicked wolf-giant Malsum. There were weird stories about the Indian devil Lox, whose mischievous habit it was to set snares for the feet of hunters and turn their arrows in mid-air so that the game went unharmed. Still other tales concerned the great magic-maker called Pulowech, the partridge.

Once Nequanis sang a very old song in a queer, minor chant. It was about Wuchowsen, the Wind Blower, a kind of huge bird that sits on a crag at the edge of the sky and flaps his wings to make the winds blow.

When the good giant Glooskap was on earth, sang the young Indian, he once paddled out in his canoe to shoot ducks and geese along the edge of the sea. But the winds blew harder and harder so that he could barely keep afloat, much less take aim with his bow.

"Wuchowsen, the Great Bird, has done this," said Glooskap. So he went to find him. After many suns, he came to a pinnacle of rock and found an immense white bird perched on its summit.

"Grandfather," said Glooskap, "be gentler with your wings. The wind you make is too strong."

But the great bird answered: "I have been here since the beginning and I moved my wings before anything else moved in the world. I shall move my wings as I please."

Then Glooskap was angry. He rose until his head touched the clouds. He grasped the bird-giant Wuchowsen as if he were no bigger than a pigeon, tied his wings and dropped him into a deep hole in the rocks.

After that the Indians could go anywhere in their canoes

88

for the wind never blew. But soon the waters grew stagnant. The lakes were thick with scum so that even Glooskap could hardly paddle through them.

Remembering Wuchowsen, he went back to the rocky chasm and pulled out the great bird. He untied one of his wings and set him back upon his lofty rock. And always since that day the winds have blown again, but never as fiercely as in the ancient times.

Most of the legends were like that—strange, childlike fables which the Indians more than half believed. They were unlike anything Dave had ever heard, but he enjoyed listening because they took his mind off the long, weary miles.

VIII

THEY walked for six days. The trail threaded through swamps so choked with undergrowth, so filled with treacherous bog-holes, that a white man without a guide would have been hopelessly mired in the first hundred yards. Yet Cochequa led them on at a steady pace, mile after mile, and they emerged almost dry-shod.

After the swamps they climbed to higher ground, laboring over and around jutting ledges and tangles of fallen timber. The morning sun came over the hills ahead and to the right, so Dave knew they were still headed northeast. Their progress was steady, twenty miles or more between dawn and dusk each day. And they were given barely enough dry food to keep them going.

Only once, late in the afternoon of the fourth day, did they break the march. The chief found fresh deer signs crossing their trail. He left them there, taking one other hunter with him, and followed the track northward into

THEY CAME TO THE BANKS OF A NARROW, TWISTING RIVER

the dense spruce bush. Half an hour later they heard the distant crack of a musket shot. Before dark the two Indians were back with the carcass of a young doe.

That was the only fresh meat they had on their journey and it lasted for only two meals. As usual the warriors gorged themselves, preferring to carry the food in their stomachs rather than on their backs.

The country was full of streams and ponds, but until the sixth day they had avoided them. At last they came to the banks of a narrow, twisting river, its black water clogged with brush and fallen trees. Instead of crossing it, the trail swung to the left, following the shore.

Cochequa waved his arm, beckoning them on, and quickened the pace almost to a trot. It was a snakelike trail, winding through thickets of spruce and alder, sometimes close to the water's edge, sometimes high above on the rocky ridges.

Sunset came and it began to grow dark but the young chief would not let them stop. If anything he pushed on faster, so that even the braves were panting when at last they heard the sound of rushing water ahead.

In the dusk they stumbled out of the woods on the bank of a larger stream. Above and below, as far as the eye could reach, was tumbling white water.

"The Chaudière," said Nequanis. "That is a French word, but it means the same as ours—the boiling kettle. Very bad water for canoes."

They made camp on the high ground along the shore, ate

a little corn and dried meat, and rolled up in their blankets. The roar of the hurrying river was in Dave's ears when he went to sleep. When he woke next morning it was again the first thing he heard.

There was a deep eddy just below the camping place and some of the braves were fishing there while others built a fire. They breakfasted on fresh-caught trout. Half an hour later four small canoes had been brought down from carefully hidden racks in the spruce bush.

These craft were less than twenty feet long, big enough to hold only four. One prisoner was placed in each canoe, so that for the first time Dave and Nancy were separated. The girl rode in the chief's canoe and Dave was in the one steered by Nequanis.

It was ticklish work launching the birch-bark boats and loading them. Matawassie stood knee-deep in foaming water, holding the gunwale while the others took their places. Then he jumped lightly in beside Dave and the canoe shot out into the current.

That was an exciting day. Before it was over they had traversed more than forty miles of river, nearly every mile of it white water. Many times the frail craft had come close to swamping. Once Dave's canoe was hung up on a sharp rock and would surely have been broken in two if he and Matawassie had not leaped overboard into the torrent and lifted it free.

They went ashore before sunset and built a big fire, for all of the party were wet and cold and some of the duffel had to be dried out. Dave's blanket was still damp that night, but the weather had turned warmer and he slept in reasonable comfort.

They were out of the rapids by midmorning of the next day. The river still flowed swiftly but there was only an occasional stretch of white water. At noon the canoes left the shadow of the forest and glided down between tilled fields and green pastures. Dave had been in the trackless wilderness so long that he rubbed his eyes in amazement. Along the right bank ran a road and on it he saw a high-wheeled cart, drawn by fat white oxen. A man in a red wool cap sat on top of the load of hay that filled the cart. He waved and grinned as the Indians went by.

A few minutes later they passed a group of low, white-washed farm buildings with thatched roofs. A dog rushed out to bark at them and three or four children, playing on the bank, yelled a greeting in French.

It was strange indeed to find a country where white farmers and painted red savages regarded each other as friends. Dave wondered whether the French had not been wiser than the English in their method of getting along with the Indian tribes.

All afternoon they moved through settled country, with more clearings than woods bordering the river. These French Canadians had been here a long time, as their solidly built houses and prosperous herds of cattle showed. Every few miles there was a chapel of stone or hewn timber, with a cross mounted at one end of its high-peaked roof.

In the early evening they paddled up to a landing before a small village. Leaving the prisoners in the canoes, Cochequa took one other brave with him and went up the rutted road to the largest house in the settlement. When they returned their arms were filled with provisions—a sack of meal, five or six long loaves of bread, half a cheese and other foods that made Dave's mouth water.

It was still light enough to see clearly. A dozen people, men, women and children, came trooping down to stare at the canoes. They laughed and jabbered in French, pointing to the prisoners and examining the scalps held up by the warriors.

The women were inclined to make a fuss over Nancy, but when one of them would have put an arm around her the chief spoke sharply and the canoes pushed out into the stream. They paddled on for a mile or two and were well clear of the village before they camped for the night.

That supper by the bank of the Chaudière was one that Dave remembered a long time. Though he didn't know it then, it was the last real white man's food he was to taste for months and months. The crusty French bread, made of white flour, the cheese and the smoke-cured bacon brought him a sharp pang of homesickness for the kitchen back in Dover. He wondered whether his family, sitting around the table in that firelit room, had heard of the massacre on the Contoocook. Even if the news had reached them, they would have no way of knowing whether he was alive or dead. Nor did he have any means of letting them know. With such

96

thoughts in his head, it was a long time before he got to sleep that night.

Late the next afternoon the canoes skirted the high bluffs of Point Levis, and beyond them sighted the waters of a river so wide that Dave could hardly believe his eyes. It was covered with whitecaps now, for a brisk wind was blowing from the west. On the farther side, miles away, the gray towers of a city crowned a lofty promontory, and Nequanis told him it was the fortress of Quebec, the capital and heart of French Canada.

"Will you take us there?" Dave asked in his halting Abenaki.

The young Indian didn't think so. "Quebec is not a good place," he said. "They give warriors brandy to drink, then they cheat them. When our people are drunk they grow foolish. They trade many beaver for one bottle of brandy. When we get ready to sell prisoners we send a message to the French and they come to us."

"You mean you're going to sell us?" Dave asked, divided between hope and fear.

The Indian shrugged. "Sell some, keep some," he replied. "The small white girl might bring guns and powder and money. You—not so much. You belong to Matawassie and me. Maybe we keep you with us—make an Abenaki of you."

He grinned and Dave felt better. He knew that if he were sold to a Frenchman there was a chance he might be ransomed, though that would cost his father all the money he could raise or borrow. On the other hand his lot might be much worse among the French than with the Indians, and there would be less chance to escape.

They went ashore and made camp in a grove of poplars at the foot of the bluff. Half a mile beyond the place where they landed, there was a French garrison, occupying a small log fort. They heard the boom of the sunset gun, and a few minutes later three soldiers approached their fire. The leader was dressed in the white tailed-coat and cockade-trimmed hat of a French officer. His boots were polished and there were ruffles of fine linen at his throat.

While he was still some distance away, Dave saw the officer sniff somewhat disdainfully and wrinkle his nose as if the odor of an Indian encampment offended his delicate nostrils. But as he drew nearer he put on a flattering smile. He made some remark to the two soldiers who followed him, then addressed the young leader in bad Abenaki.

"Welcome, Chief," he said. "We see you have had good hunting. We are glad."

Cochequa stood erect and dignified, his face expressing neither pleasure nor dislike.

"It is as the French Chief says," he replied. "We have hunted well. We have taken seven scalps and these four prisoners. Now we go back to our lodges on the River of the Wolves."

The French officer nodded and sauntered among them. He gave the scalps only a perfunctory scrutiny but looked with more interest at the prisoners. Dave saw him stare at Nancy and realized with a jolt of fear that she might be taken away. Then he noticed that her face was smeared with dirt and her yellow hair matted with cockle-burrs and sticks. The brave who had captured her seemed surprised at this sudden transformation, but said nothing.

Nancy scowled at the officer and made a face, whereupon he laughed carelessly and turned away. He looked longer at Judith Gray. A little color had come back into her white face during the journey and since she had eaten more regularly she was no longer the walking skeleton she had once appeared. But the haggard, haunted look was still in her eyes.

The Frenchman gave her straight figure an appraising stare and felt of her thin arm, much as if he were a farmer judging a horse. At last he shrugged and swung about on his heel. For Dave and Josh Boles he spared no more than a passing glance. Apparently he was not interested in buying any prisoners.

Observing the formalities, the officer wished Cochequa a polite good evening, offered him a pinch of snuff and took his departure.

When the Frenchmen were out of hearing, Nequanis muttered something to Matawassie which led Dave to believe the Indians were not too pleased with this visit. No presents had been given them, and there had been no invitation to call at the garrison. From the gruff way in which they treated their captives that night, the boy could see that their pride had been offended.

The next morning was warm and bright, and the braves

were in better humor as they loaded the canoes. This time they gave special attention to the stowing of the duffel. Bundles were rolled tightly and a deerskin cover was tied down over the cargo in each canoe.

Dave discovered the reason for these precautions as soon as the little fleet had passed from the mouth of the Chaudière into the St. Lawrence. What had seemed no more than a gentle breeze while they were in the smaller stream turned out to be a lusty southwest wind on the broad river. It blew from almost astern as they swung northeastward along the shore. White-crested waves ran merrily past them and it required skillful paddling to keep the canoes from shipping water.

Dave had plenty of opportunity to look at the gray city on the opposite hill and at the full-rigged ships, brigs and schooners anchored in the roadstead. It was his first glimpse of a big, important town. He had never been to Boston, and the little harbor of Portsmouth shrank to insignificance in comparison with Quebec.

The river was a busy place that morning. Bateaux and barges loaded with produce from the farms moved sluggishly across the current, heading for the city markets. A weatherbeaten ship from France came beating up the channel, her crew lining the forward rail. They yelled and pointed at sight of the Indian canoes.

After an hour's paddling, Dave saw a huge island dividing the river ahead. They took the southern channel, which was itself several miles wide, and all morning long the shore of the island rose on their left. With the breeze behind them they were making good time. As nearly as the boy could judge, they had traveled twenty miles when the sun showed it was noon.

Beyond the end of the big island the river opened out so wide that he could barely see the northern shore. He was not surprised when he tasted a drop of the water and found it almost as salty as the ocean.

For several hours they had had an ebbing tide to help them. Now, shortly after midday, it began to run strongly upstream and the result was a choppy sea that tossed the canoes about like corks. They bore to the right, paddling hard, and finally made their way into a sheltered cove on the southern shore.

After half a day in the cramped quarters of the canoe, Dave was glad to stretch his legs on land. He walked about, waiting for the sun to dry his spray-drenched clothes, and Nancy Morrison joined him. Her face was clean now, and her hair combed and shining.

"You sure look a lot better'n you did last night," Dave laughed. "What happened to you?"

"I fixed myself up to look ugly when I saw that Frenchman coming," the girl replied. "I didn't want him to buy me, because I'd rather stay with you. We're still going to run away, aren't we, David? And you're going to take me home. Promise?"

"Yes," said Dave soberly. "I promise."

IX

THE SOUTHWEST wind held, and when the tide turned, just before sunset, the canoes put out once more. They paddled until late in the evening and covered another ten or fifteen miles before they camped.

It was not yet dawn when Nequanis shook Dave awake. "We go soon," he told the white boy. "When the sun rises the water will run toward the sea."

Dave built a fire and Nequanis made johnny-cakes of corn meal, which he baked on a flat stone, heated in the coals. Matawassie meanwhile had caught several small fish, of a kind unfamiliar to Dave, and they had a more elaborate breakfast than usual.

There was hardly any breeze when they got into the canoes, but the tide was past the flood and they were soon driving along at four or five miles an hour. More wooded islands appeared to the north. Every few miles there was a glimpse of low, white houses on the mainland shore.

From one of these French villages, late in the morning, they saw two big canoes shoot out. There were four men in each, paddling hard and singing lustily as they skimmed along. They passed within a hundred yards, heading northward toward a gap between two islands. Dave could not understand the words of their song, but the rollicking lilt of it and the bright colors of their costumes gave him a feeling of excitement and adventure.

Their blanket-cloth shirts were vivid blue, and they wore red sashes and red knitted caps with tassels that swung rakishly at the side. Their canoes were loaded deep with provisions and duffel.

"They are what the French call *'hivernants,'*" Nequanis explained. "Winterers. They go now to a place far up the Saguenay to trap and trade for furs. They will stay there many moons, until the snow melts and the ice goes out of the rivers."

At noon the Indian party went ashore again to wait for a favoring tide. Later, as before, they went on through the evening and put a long stretch of river behind them. Dave thought they must have come eighty or ninety miles in the two days since they left the Chaudière.

The third morning dawned bleak and cloudy, with a northerly wind that made paddling difficult. Even with the tide to help them, they were constantly buffeted by waves that slopped over the port gunwale and threatened to swing the bow off course.

It was grim work, but Dave could sense the same eagerness

in the Indians' paddling that he had noticed when they approached the Co-hos intervales. Every mile they gained was bringing them nearer to their home lodges.

That night around the campfire the young braves spent hours daubing their faces with fresh paint, applied with painstaking care. The sober concentration they gave to this task made Dave smile. He was reminded of his older sister Jane, primping for a party. But at the same time he was sure now that they must be close to the River of the Wolves.

When morning came it was fair and still, a perfect early fall day. Reckoning back on his fingers, Dave decided it must be either the last day of August or the first of September, though he could not be sure which.

They got off to an early start and paddled fast with a helping tide. Young Matawassie was humming happily as he swung his blade—a long, tuneless Abenaki chant.

It was just noon when Nequanis gave a whoop of triumph and heaved on the steering paddle, turning the bow toward the wooded shore. In a few minutes they had rounded a point, shaggy with pines and spruces, and were moving up the channel of a narrow, swift-flowing river.

The Indian town was four miles inland from the mouth of the stream. Dave's first glimpse of it came as a surprise, for he had imagined something wilder and more picturesque. Clustered along the bank in a clearing were some thirty houses—not wigwams but square-built huts of logs and poles, chinked with moss and roofed with bark. They stood at various angles instead of lined up along a street, as they would have been in a New England village. At one end of the group of buildings, and a little apart, was a tiny log church with a white cross on top.

As soon as they were within sight of the town, Cochequa lifted his musket and fired it into the air. At the echoing report dogs began to bark and a dozen squaws, a swarm of children and a few old men came running to the bank.

They waded into the water, seizing the gunwales of the canoes in the eagerness of their welcome and chattering like a flock of blackbirds in cherry time.

Dave was dragged bodily out on the bank and hustled up the steep slope. He found himself standing with the other prisoners in a wide cleared space in the middle of the village. It was a kind of town square, irregular in shape and trampled almost as hard as a brick pavement. After the Indians had satisfied their first curiosity as to the white captives, they turned to the warriors and began asking questions.

Dave had a chance to look around him. The houses were less impressive, seen from this level. They looked small and dirty and a smell of rancid grease and wood smoke came from them. There was no glass in the windows. Either they were empty black holes or covered by ragged deerskin, scraped to paper thinness and painted with crude, bright drawings of animals.

On poles in front of several of the cabins bits of hair fluttered in the breeze. They were scalps, Dave realized with a shudder—weather-worn trophies of past expeditions.

At one side of the open space a section of a log, three or

four feet in diameter, stood on end, its top covered by a tight-laced piece of rawhide. It looked like a huge drum, and when the boy edged close enough to tap on its head a hollow rumbling sound came forth. He guessed then that the square had been beaten smooth by the feet of braves, doing their tribal dances to the accompaniment of the great drum.

The prisoners had been standing there for nearly half an hour when the jabber of the Indians was suddenly hushed. A figure in a long, flapping black robe was striding toward them from the direction of the chapel.

Cochequa separated himself from the crowd and turned to meet the newcomer.

"Father Pierre," he murmured, and bobbed his head respectfully.

The priest held out a thin, work-worn hand and grasped the hand of the young chief.

"We are glad to welcome you back, my son," he said in good Abenaki. "But not all of you have returned. The others —are they safe?"

"All safe," Cochequa answered. "One, only, has gone to the Happy Hunting Grounds." And he explained that some of the party had stayed in the Co-hos country to wait for the corn harvest.

Father Pierre nodded and a smile of relief passed momentarily over his pale, lined face. He came toward the little group of prisoners. Instinctively Dave felt a kind of sympathy for the gaunt, lonely man. He had never seen a

HE MADE THE SIGN OF BENEDICTION OVER THEM

pair of eyes that held such sadness.

With an effort the priest began to speak in slow, queer-sounding English.

"My cheeldren," he said. "Do not be on'appy. You weel be treat' well 'ere. You are not of my Church, but come to me eef you 'ave troubles."

He crossed himself, murmured a few words of Latin and made the sign of benediction over them. Then he turned and strode away toward the little church. The silence was broken as soon as he passed inside the door. The squaws gabbled louder than ever, talking so fast that Dave could understand only a few words here and there.

Half a dozen lean mongrel dogs wandered through the crowd, sniffing curiously at the captives. One of them, a big, tawny-colored animal that had the head and ears of a wolf, came close to Dave and stood looking up at him with intelligent amber eyes.

The boy put out his hand and touched the brute's head. At first he felt a shiver of fear go through the dog, but when his fingers began scratching behind the ears, the animal moved closer, rubbing against his knees, tongue lolling blissfully.

Dave grinned. "I guess we're going to be friends, aren't we, boy?" he said in English. "What's your name, huh? Got to have a name. I'll call you Buck. How's that? Like it, Buck?"

The dog looked pleased and took a quick lick at Dave's hand. But at that moment Matawassie pushed Buck out of the way with a careless swing of his moccasined foot.

"Come," he told the white boy. "We go to the sweat-house. Tonight, when the hunters come back there will be a feast and dancing. We must be clean."

Nequanis joined them and they went through the village to a small wigwam of bark and skins, standing close to the river bank. It was barely large enough to hold the three of them, for a big kettle filled the center of the earth floor. It was half full of water, and sprigs of pennyroyal and other herbs floated on the surface.

The two young braves stripped off their leggins and moccasins and Dave followed their example, tossing his clothes outside as they had done. A moment later he was embarrassed when the flap of the wigwam opened and two giggling squaws shouldered in. They were carrying large stones, heated at the village campfire, holding them on smoking sticks. The stones were dropped with a sizzle and a splash into the kettle and the squaws ducked out again. Dave could hear their voices outside, as they gathered up the clothing and carried it off. They were still chattering about his white skin.

Meanwhile the wigwam had filled quickly with pungent steam. He could feel the sweat starting from every pore in his body. The Indians grunted with pleasure, and in the darkness he heard them rubbing themselves and slapping their wet skin.

The steam bath lasted perhaps a quarter of an hour. Then Nequanis burst out through the entrance flap and sprinted to the top of the bank, taking off in a long, flat dive. Matawassie and Dave were close on his heels. The shock of the cold water made the white boy gasp, but he struck out strongly and felt a tingling glow shoot through his veins. It was as if the cleansing steam had drawn the sluggishness out of him and given him new vigor.

He whooped exuberantly with the Indian lads and when they swam ashore he raced them to the bank. Fresh, clean clothing was waiting for them there. Dave put on a loin-cloth, a pair of deerskin leggins and tough moose-hide moccasins that were better than the ones he had been wearing. Around his naked upper body he wrapped his blanket, following the example of his companions.

About the time they were dressed, Bemokis and Josh Boles came out of the sweat-house. Josh was stubborn about plunging into the river. When he refused to dive, the bent-backed Indian seized him by the hair, dragged him down the bank and ducked him in the chilly water.

Josh sputtered and struggled but was finally persuaded to swim a few strokes. Nequanis watched him, scowling.

"He is a bad prisoner," the young warrior told Dave. "He will make trouble for himself."

They went up through the village, Dave feeling somewhat conspicuous in his Indian dress. But nobody paid much attention to him. The braves were squatted in the doorways of their cabins renewing their warpaint. The squaws had gone back to their work in the little corn and pumpkin patches that lay between the houses and the edge of the woods.

Nequanis and Matawassie led the way to the smallest and most dilapidated hut in the town. It was at the farther end of the row, only a few yards from the chapel and the priest's house. Dave gathered from the Indians' talk that this was one of several cabins used as bachelor quarters by the younger braves.

"You will live here with us," Nequanis told him. "You will do the squaw work—getting wood, making fires, cooking and washing. That is for now. Afterward, if you prove yourself strong and brave, perhaps the chief will let you become a hunter, as we are."

Dave took the new order of things with good grace. After all, he reflected, the chores he was expected to do were just what any white boy did in the settlements—all but the cooking, which he didn't mind. After the hard, constant labor of the journey northward, his present lot seemed an easy one.

Since he had nothing else to do while the young braves were decorating themselves, he took an ax and followed the path into the forest. In an hour he had cut up half a dozen dead trees and brought back the wood to stack behind the cabin. Then he started to build a fire, but Nequanis told him it was not needed.

"There will be a big campfire tonight," said the Indian, "and much eating. Our chief, Maranoquid, the father of Cochequa, has been on a hunt with the other men of the town. Soon they will come back with meat. If they have made a good kill, some of the meat will be smoked and dried for winter. But there will be enough left over for a feast."

It was about two hours before sunset when a high-pitched Indian war whoop came from the river above the town. The dogs began barking furiously and everybody in the village hurried toward the landing.

Dave saw six canoes coming swiftly downstream. There were four Indians in each one, and they shouted, waved their paddles and pointed to the carcasses of deer and moose that loaded the birch-bark craft deep in the water.

The first man ashore was a stalwart six-foot redskin with mighty shoulders. He wore three eagle feathers in his scalplock, and a long necklace of bears' claws about his neck. Dave did not have to be told that this was Maranoquid, the chief.

Neither the older man nor Cochequa, his son, gave any special sign of joy as they greeted each other. Each had the grave and courteous manner expected of a leader. Maranoquid asked no questions about the war party, nor did Cochequa inquire as to the success of the hunt. Indeed, no one would have needed to ask. The heavily loaded canoes spoke for themselves.

The braves carried the bodies of four deer, a moose, a black bear and some smaller game to the top of the bank, where the squaws immediately set to work with their skinning knives. No rules of behavior governed their tongues and they kept up a running fire of talk and laughter while they ripped the hides off the animals and cut up the meat.

The hearts, livers, tongues and other Indian delicacies were put in one pile for immediate cooking. The tougher parts of the carcasses were saved for winter food. But nothing seemed to be wasted. The sinews and intestines—even the hoofs and claws—were carefully removed. Dave knew that they would be used later for stitching clothes, making bow-strings, bags and ornaments.

He went back to the cabin where Nequanis and Mata-wassie were waiting. They sat cross-legged, wearing such finery as they owned and looking proud and satisfied. The bright new stripes of pigment on their faces made them extra hideous—extra handsome, Dave supposed, to Indian eyes.

"When the feast starts," Nequanis told him soberly, "if you are wise you will not eat too much. You may have to do some running afterwards, and it will be better for you if you can run fast."

The young brave glanced at Matawassie, and Dave thought he caught the flicker of a grin under the streaks of paint.

X

A S DARKNESS crept over the town the great drum began to beat. Dave heard the throb of it and looked out to see what was happening. A dozen squaws were busy around a big cook-fire, stirring kettles and roasting meat on spits. Beyond the immediate circle of light made by the fire, everything looked unreal and shadowy, but an occasional gleam fell on the drum and the strange figure standing behind it. Dave made out the shape of a man, his face painted with weird vertical stripes of yellow. Above his eyes was the grinning head of a wolf, the long white teeth glittering wickedly when the firelight touched them. The wolfskin hung over the man's shoulders but his bare arms moved up and down in rhythm as he struck the taut hide with the flat of his hands.

"That," Nequanis said, from the darkness at Dave's elbow, "is the M'teoulin—the medicine man. He is very old and very wise, and familiar with all the spirits."

The throb of the drum quickened and grew louder. One by one the warriors came out of their houses and went toward the fire. When Maranoquid, the chief, arrived, he dipped his hand in the huge stew kettle, drew out a piece of meat and began eating it. After that they all fell to without further ceremony.

Mindful of Nequanis' advice, Dave did not gorge himself, good as the food tasted. He tried to warn Josh Boles, who was stuffing himself with fat chunks of bear and raccoon meat, but the other boy merely scowled and ate faster.

For nearly an hour the feast went on. At last, when the braves were full almost to bursting, they seated themselves in a circle around the fire and the chief lighted a stone pipe. The pungent smoke of tobacco and kinnikinnick drifted in a wreath above his eagle crest. When he had taken two or three puffs he passed the pipe to Cochequa and it went on around the circle.

The squaws and the prisoners sat in an outer ring, and still farther from the fire the dogs sniffed and trotted back and forth, scavenging for scraps. Father Pierre was not there. A beam of candlelight, coming from the window of the little church, showed where he knelt at his prayers. The medicine man, on the other hand, was much in evidence. He had left the drum when the feasting began and now he strutted about near the fire, calling on various spirits, gesturing with his skinny arms and doing small feats of magic. He would hold a birch twig in one hand, make a pass over it and cause it to disappear. Dave was not impressed, for he had seen more than one white man who was better at such tricks than the old Indian.

After a while Maranoquid rose and began to speak in the measured sing-song cadence that was typical of the Abenaki ceremonial language. As his deep voice rolled out the sentences, Dave realized it was a kind of poetry.

The chief described the hunt in detail, telling how they had gone up the river; how the first deer had been sighted by such-and-such a warrior; how so-and-so had fired and missed because Lox, the evil one, had turned the bullet in mid-air. The tale ran on and on till all the game was accounted for and loaded in the canoes.

When Maranoquid finished he turned politely to his son and asked for an account of the war party's experiences.

Cochequa was not the orator his father was, but he spoke well. Dave heard for the first time that the raiding band had attacked two other small settlements near the Connecticut before they reached the Contoocook. As each incident was told, the proper scalp or prisoner was trotted out for inspection. The young chief was fairly modest about his own deeds, but he played up the exploits of Bemokis, making the Indian with the twisted back the principal hero of the expedition.

When Cochequa held up the red scalp and told the story of the looting and burning of the Foster farm, Dave had to hold himself tense to keep from shaking. Then the chief's son turned in his direction and he was seized and led into the circle by his two young captors. He walked stiffly, his back straight and his lips tight. Several of the older warriors grunted their approval of Nequanis and Matawassie for taking him prisoner, and he felt the whole ring of beady eyes centered on him for a long moment. Then he was hustled out again and the narrative continued.

It was now well along toward midnight and there was a chill in the air. The fire had been kept up, but it gave little warmth beyond the inner circle of braves. The squaws and prisoners wrapped their blankets tightly around them and sat shivering while Cochequa was winding up his oration.

The older chief rose, when his son had finished, and complimented all the members of the party on their courage and skill. Then shorter speeches were made by Bemokis and some of the other veteran warriors. And finally the M'teoulin pronounced a few incantations, whirled about in a fantastic dance and appeared to vanish in a puff of smoke.

Dave stared at the place where the sorcerer had stood. Most of the Indians seemed as mystified as he was, but the older braves chuckled and applauded. After a moment the big drum, back in the darkness, began to rumble. Peering behind him, Dave was not surprised to see the wolf mask of the medicine man bobbing above the drumhead.

As the throb of the beat grew faster, the young bucks leaped up and began to prance. Bending from the waist and throwing their knees high, they picked up the rhythm of the drum with their pounding moccasins. One by one other warriors jumped to their feet, until only Chief Maranoquid and a dozen of the more venerable men were left seated.

THE BOOMING OF THE DRUM QUICKENED IN TEMPO

The booming of the drum quickened in tempo, and the dancing grew wilder as the young braves shouted hoarsely and flung their arms above their heads. Dave caught the fierce excitement. He felt his blood beat faster, in time with the drum's thunder. At the climax, he even wished he could get up there and join in the dance.

At last the warriors had enough. Panting, their copper bodies glistening with sweat, they flung themselves down on their blankets. The pipe went around the circle again. When it reached Bemokis he got to his feet and pointed the reed stem toward the prisoners. Dave could not hear clearly what he said, for his words were drowned out by gleeful whoops and cheers.

All the younger braves sprang up and ran toward their houses. When they came back, each one was carrying a kind of flattened club, three or four feet long.

Dave caught his breath. He understood now what Nequanis had been talking about before the feast. The prisoners—or at least Josh Boles and he—were going to have to run the gantlet!

Ever since he was a child he had heard tales of how the Indians put their male captives to this form of torture. Boys, and even grown men, had been beaten to death in the gantlet, according to stories told in the settlements. The clubs appeared brutal enough, but he could tell by the way the young men swung them that they were lighter than they looked. Probably they were made of spruce.

The braves lined up in a double row, a dozen on a side.

Nequanis and Matawassie came toward Dave and another pair of Indians approached Josh Boles. The two boys had their leggins stripped off and were led toward the head of the lane of yelling braves.

Bemokis was the first Indian in line, and he brandished his long club, his cruel face grinning with anticipation. Dave, standing there shivering in his breechclout, set his teeth and waited. Bemokis pointed at him.

"Let that one run first!" he shouted, and the others greeted his words with a cheer.

Dave felt himself pushed forward. A sudden desperate resolve took form in his head. He had been afraid, but now his fear was gone in a surge of bright anger. He started running at top speed. Then, just as he flashed abreast of Bemokis, he swerved straight at him.

The Indian with the twisted back had both arms lifted high, ready to strike a mighty blow. Dave's shoulder caught him squarely in the stomach and doubled him up with his wind knocked out. The boy was lucky then. As the club flew out of Bemokis' fingers he caught it in mid-air. It felt good in his hands—smooth, well-balanced, heavy enough to do damage if it landed in the right places. He whirled the club around his head, parried a glancing blow from the Indian across the way and struck savagely at the next brave in line. Then he raced down the alley, whaling away to right and left as he ran.

He was hit solidly half a dozen times before he reached the other end, but he was still on his feet. Fully expecting the angry mob to follow him, he dashed on another fifty yards before he came to a panting stop. Nobody was near him. He turned and saw the whole crowd roaring and rolling on the ground with laughter.

Nequanis had left the line and was hurrying to meet him. The young Indian had a lump over one eye but he grinned broadly as he slapped Dave on the back.

"You did what I hoped you would do, my Brother," he said. "Even Bemokis must agree now that you have courage."

As they walked back the lines were forming again. The bent-backed Indian had picked up another club and was waiting in his place, crouching a little and wearing a ferocious scowl. Dave felt sorry for Josh Boles.

The stocky white boy was plainly scared. He hung back till a pair of braves caught him by the arms and threw him into the opening between the rows. Stumbling, he put up his arms to protect his head and started to run. The clubs rose and fell like flails—*thwack—thwack—thwack—*landing heavily on his back, shoulders and elbows. The poor lad fell twice but staggered up again and went on. He was blubbering like a baby when he passed the end of the line, and he dropped in a heap, blood oozing from half a dozen bruises on his body.

The Indians turned away from him contemptuously but Dave picked him up, wiped off the blood as best he could and helped him over to his blanket.

"Here," he said, "just lie still and they won't bother you

any more. I'll get some water and fix you up the best I can."

Dave brought a kettle from the cabin and ran down to the river. Carrying it back full of cold water he washed Josh's head and body, then wrapped his blanket around him and left him sitting there in the shadows.

It was close to midnight now but the gathering showed no signs of breaking up. Cochequa was standing before the elders of the village, making another harangue. This time he was briefer. Dave paid little attention to what he was saying, but suddenly he saw the young chief stretch out one muscular arm and point directly at him. Nequanis, too, was beckoning. Hesitantly the boy stepped forward and in a moment he was standing inside the circle of warriors, his back to the fire.

"You have seen what this young paleface has done," Cochequa chanted. "He is strong and his heart is brave. On the trail he carried his pack and did not grow weary. In the canoes he worked hard with the paddle. He is of an age when he can be taught to hunt with the skill of an Abenaki.

"Already he speaks a little in our tongue. Our young brother, Nequanis, will vouch for him and teach him. I, Cochequa, ask that you take this white youth into kinship with our tribe."

The faces of the older Indians were as expressionless as blocks of wood. Maranoquid refilled the pipe and it went the rounds while Dave stood uncomfortably in the middle of the ring. The young chief's words had taken him completely by surprise. He felt a thrill of pride when he realized that a real compliment had been paid him, but there was no telling how the warriors would react. He wasn't even sure whether he wanted to become a member of the tribe, for he recalled all too clearly the terrible scene in his uncle's clearing.

Fifteen or twenty minutes dragged by. Then Maranoquid rose slowly and with great dignity.

"Cochequa, my son, has spoken," said he. "Our numbers are few, for many of our men have fallen in battle. If this young paleface is strong and brave, as we have seen and as Cochequa has told us, he may become a true warrior of the Abenakis."

Scattered nods and grunts came from the assembled elders. Finally Bemokis stood up.

"You know me," he said. "I have hated the English since I was a boy. I have killed many and taken many scalps. But I believe this young Bostonnais has courage. I have felt the weight of his blows on my body. I, Bemokis, say he is ready to be taken into the tribe."

Those words seemed to swing the decision. One after another the warriors voiced their approval. As the last one finished speaking, the M'teoulin stalked into the center of the ring. He lifted both thin arms and uttered a scream so sudden and so piercing that Dave leaped back, startled. Then he found Nequanis beside him, steadying him.

"Do not be afraid," the Indian boy whispered. "What comes now will make you a man and an Abenaki."

The medicine man shuffled forward, muttering mysteriously. Out of his robe he whipped a slim, shining knife, and with his other hand he seized Dave's left wrist. The white boy clamped his jaws hard to keep from shivering, for the needlelike point of the knife was poised just above his open hand.

With a quick, careful movement the M'teoulin pricked the end of Dave's middle finger. Then he turned toward Nequanis, took his left hand and went through the same performance.

Mumbling more incantations the old Indian took a drop of Dave's blood on his finger and placed it on Nequanis' tongue. In a moment Dave tasted the Indian lad's blood, warm and salt, in his own mouth.

"Say these words," the medicine man commanded. "He is my brother. I am his brother."

Together the two boys repeated the Indian words.

"At all times and in all places," the M'teoulin continued, "until the squirrel again grows greater than the bear."

"At all times and in all places," they murmured in unison, "until the squirrel again grows greater than the bear."

Dave had a queer feeling, as if he were outside his body and listening to someone else speaking. Then the sorcerer leaped into the air and gave that bloodcurdling scream, and the spell was broken.

"Welcome, Brother," said Nequanis with a grin, and threw his arms around him.

DAVE woke next morning to the sound of a church bell ringing. For a moment he lay there in his ragged blanket blinking and staring at the dark log walls. The familiar sound had carried him back to Dover, where he had been wakened on so many Sunday mornings by the clear, sweet tolling of the bell in the church steeple.

Matawassie was already on his feet. Now Nequanis got up, growling and rubbing his eyes.

He nudged Dave with his toe. "Come, Brother," he said. "It is time to go to the church."

Dave jumped up and looked around for his clothes. Then he remembered that all he had was what he wore. He ran down the bank to the river, washed his hands and face and combed his hair as best he could with his fingers. The two Indian youths looked at him with disapproval when he came back. They were rubbing themselves with bear's grease from a small, smelly pot.

"When you become an Abenaki," said Nequanis, "you will learn that water is for drinking."

Dave grinned but made no reply. There were some Indian customs he hoped he would never have to learn.

They pulled their blankets around them and walked toward the chapel in company with a score of others. The little building was clean and whitewashed inside, and rows of plain wooden benches faced the altar. As they passed through the door they saw Father Pierre, lean and frail in his black robe, pulling on the bell rope.

The three boys took seats near the back. Matawassie crossed himself devoutly and Dave bowed his head for a moment. After that he had an opportunity to look about. The chapel was already more than half filled. Most of the congregation was made up of squaws and children but there was a sprinkling of the younger braves. As his eye roved over the dark heads, Dave noticed one young woman with hair of a lighter shade, and there was a little boy of seven or eight whose uncombed thatch was tow-colored—almost white. Both were dressed like Indians, but he was sure they must be white prisoners, taken in earlier raids.

Neither Nancy Morrison nor Judith Gray had been brought to the church. Josh Boles, he knew, was still stiff and weak from his beating and was probably in bed.

The service was simple and fairly short. The priest conducted most of it in Latin, but at the end he talked to them briefly in Abenaki. He was a good man, Dave thought, but sad and troubled by the waywardness of his flock. The

Indians paid small attention to the precepts of proper behavior he tried to teach, and even less to his preaching of the gospel of love. Only when he stretched out his hands to bless them did they seem impressed. This was a kind of medicine they understood.

As the crowd left the chapel, Dave had a better look at the two prisoners. The young woman was fat and stolid-looking, apparently perfectly content to be a squaw. Dave squirmed at the thought that Nancy might become like her some day, unless he could get the girl away from this place. The small boy, naked to the waist like the Indian children, was burned by the sun to a color that matched his companions' copper skin. Only his pale hair and blue eyes set him apart. Dave spoke to him in English and got nothing but a blank stare in return. The child must have been captured so young that he had no memory of the speech of his parents.

With morning Mass over, the village went back at once to its weekday routine. There were no rules for observing the Sabbath, such as Dave had known in Puritan New England. Some of the squaws set off for the fields or went into the forest to gather firewood. Others built long fires under racks of poles and began the smoking of venison and bear meat. All day the good smell of hickory smoke drifted through the town.

Nequanis and Matawassie took Dave with them and went fishing. There was a deep, still pool half a mile below the village, where big trout lay under the ledges of the bank.

They tried worms, grubs and grasshoppers for bait, but it was late afternoon before the fish began biting. Toward sunset they hooked four fat trout in quick succession and set out for home.

Matawassie was sour-faced and sulky. He had been silent all afternoon, but now he said something to Nequanis that made the other boy stop and put down his string of fish. Dave, coming up behind, realized that the argument was about himself.

The fact that Dave had been made a blood brother of Nequanis had roused an old jealousy between the two. Matawassie believed he should have the credit for capturing the white boy and he stated his claim now with some bitterness.

"Brother," Nequanis answered him calmly, "you and I have been brothers since we were no bigger than chipmunks. It is wrong that we should quarrel now. Cochequa, Bemokis and the others decided that the young paleface should become my brother. If you have the better right to teach him and make him a warrior, I will give him over to you. I will wrestle you now, to see which of us is the stronger and will be the better teacher."

As he finished speaking, Matawassie flung down his fishing pole and sprang toward him, eyes flashing. Nequanis was a little the bigger of the two, but Matawassie was lightning-fast. They locked arms, each straining to throw the other off balance. Their feet moved in and out with catlike speed. There was no sound but their panting and the rustle of

HE THREW MATAWASSIE SIDEWISE, BUT THE YOUNG INDIAN
TWISTED IN THE AIR, LITHE AS A SNAKE

their moccasins among the leaves.

After a moment Nequanis shot out a leg and hooked it behind his opponent's knee. With a heave he threw Matawassie sidewise, but the young Indian twisted in the air, lithe as a snake. They struck the ground together and for an instant Dave thought Matawassie had squirmed on top. Then he saw that Nequanis had a powerful arm locked around the younger lad's neck. With a rolling motion he turned Matawassie on his back and made his weight count as he pinned the boy's slim shoulders to the earth. Struggle as he would, Matawassie was beaten and he knew it.

Nequanis stood up, breathing hard but smiling. He reached out a hand, and after a second's hesitation Matawassie took it. The boy got to his feet, stood there a moment scowling at the ground, then snatched up his pole and started toward the town without a word to either of them.

Nequanis turned to Dave with a shrug. "He has eaten bitter medicine," he said. "Come. We have much to do before we sleep. Tomorrow we go on a hunt, Brother— you and I."

.　　　.　　　.　　　.　　　.　　　.　　　.

The sun was barely up when they got into the light canoe. Dave took the bow paddle and Nequanis steered in the stern. Amidships their duffel was neatly stowed—blankets, bows and arrows, fishing tackle and enough corn and jerked meat to last them five days.

Each boy had a knife and a tomahawk at his waist, and the young Indian also carried a woodchuck-skin pouch that held a clamshell, filled with smoldering punk. It was hard for Dave to believe that fire could be kept alive for a whole day in such a contrivance, but Nequanis assured him it had been done for generations, long before the white man brought his flint and steel to the country.

This hunt, the Indian boy insisted, was to be made in the old way. No guns or other newfangled inventions would be taken. It was time, he told Dave sternly, for the white captive to learn a little woodcraft and to accustom himself to hardship as every young warrior must do.

As they pushed out from the shore Dave saw Nancy Morrison coming down the bank to get water. She was dressed in a doeskin shirt and breeches like those worn by the squaws, and she carried a clay water pot half as big as herself.

He waved to her and she waved back.

"We're going hunting," Dave called. "I'll bring you back a present."

The girl laughed. "Good-bye!" she said. "I hope you'll be lucky."

A moment later they rounded a bend and she was hidden from sight by the woods. Dave felt a tingle of excitement as the dark, unbroken forest stretched ahead. He thought he was going to enjoy this outing. He started to hum a little tune under his breath, but Nequanis silenced him with a gruff order.

"We are on a hunt," said the Indian. "From this time on we make no noise. Chattering and singing is for jays and squirrels. The moose, the deer and the bear are quiet.''

The canoe slipped onward through smooth stretches where the sunlight dappled the water and through fast-flowing riffles where the stream foamed white around rocks.

Dave bent his back to the task and paddled hard, and before noon they had made fifteen miles up the river. Suddenly the boy felt the canoe swing to the left and they cut in swiftly toward the bank.

Nequanis caught hold of an overhanging bough and steadied the craft in the current. Looking around, Dave saw him pointing to a slanting stretch of clay, two or three feet high. The foot of it was in the water and at the top of its smooth length was a hole, going back into the bank. The slippery surface of the clay was wet from top to bottom.

The young Indian put his finger to his lips in a warning gesture. Carefully, so as to make no splash, he dipped his paddle and worked the canoe forward another hundred yards. There he tied the craft to a tree and they went quietly ashore. Nequanis picked up his bow and motioned to Dave to do the same. Then they crept back along the high ground to a place just above the clay bank.

The white boy had never seen an otter slide, but he had heard trappers talk about them and he felt sure this must be one. Nequanis signaled him to stay where he was and crawled down the slope on his belly, silent as a snake. It took the Indian boy three or four minutes to cover a dozen yards. At the end of that time he eased himself up to a sitting position, strung his bow and fitted an arrow to the string. Then he sat perfectly still and waited.

It seemed to Dave as if hours passed. It took all his will power to keep from moving. A mosquito came out of nowhere and hummed annoyingly around his head. Like Nequanis, he wore only a loincloth and moccasins, and the twigs tickled his bare legs. Once he had an almost uncontrollable desire to sneeze.

Just when he thought he could stand the waiting no longer, he saw Nequanis begin to pull back on the bowstring. The Indian was leaning forward a little, the muscles of his back and shoulders bunching under the tawny skin. Then the bow twanged and the young brave leaped to his feet with an exultant yell.

Dave ran down to join him. Thrashing about in the water below the slide was a long, sleek body, covered with dark fur. The shaft of the arrow was driven clear through it.

Nequanis sprang down the bank and finished the otter with a blow of his tomahawk. His face wore a look of pride as he carried the animal back to the canoe.

"This is good medicine," he told Dave. "It is a sign we shall have a good hunt. The skin of an otter is worth four beaver."

He proceeded to strip off the pelt, careful not to damage the glossy fur. While they were at work the Indian looked up suddenly and scowled. Out of the woods trotted the big yellow dog that had made friends with Dave on his first day in the village. He came toward them cautiously, uncertain of his welcome, a hopeful grin at the corners of his mouth.

"Get out!" Nequanis snarled. "Go home, worthless one!"

"Wait," Dave begged. "Perhaps he can help us. Don't you ever use dogs to hunt?"

The Indian shrugged. "Dogs trained for bear and raccoon —yes. But this one is a stray. He came to our village from nobody knows where. He will only frighten the game."

"Why not try him?" Dave argued. "Maybe he was trained to hunt. And this otter meat is no good to us. We can feed him on that."

"You beg like a woman," Nequanis growled. "But I will let him follow us for one day. If he makes a noise I will kill him."

Dave had to be satisfied with this compromise. He scratched the dog's eager head.

"Look here, Buck," he said soberly. "You heard what'll happen to you if you do any barking. Better watch how you behave."

They gave the dog part of the otter's carcass. Dave cut up the rest and wrapped it in leaves while Nequanis rolled the skin in a bundle. Then they got back into the canoe.

Dave had eaten nothing since his early breakfast but he was used to the Indian custom of two meals a day now. As they paddled on up the river he caught occasional glimpses of the dog, trotting like a silent shadow among the trees. About sunset Nequanis beached the canoe and they fished a deep pool at the foot of a rapid. The trout were rising well. Before dusk they had half a dozen beauties for their supper.

Buck sat on his haunches, back among the trees, and watched them prepare the meal. His pink tongue drooled at the smell of the sizzling fish. But when they had finished and were ready to turn in, the dog had disappeared.

The two boys sat by the dying fire awhile, talking in low voices. Nequanis was telling Dave about the habits of the otter, the mink and the beaver. He reached for his blanket at last, and was about to roll up in it, when a short, deep bark sounded from the forest.

With a muttered exclamation of anger the Indian snatched up his hatchet, his purpose all too plain. And Dave followed him unhappily into the woods.

STUMBLING along in the darkness, the boy heard the dog's bark repeated. It sounded urgent and expectant, as if Buck were listening for a reply. Nequanis, in the lead, said nothing, but his steps had quickened. Then, after two or three minutes, he suddenly paused and put out a warning hand to stop Dave.

"The dog has treed a raccoon," he whispered. "See—up there in the branches. Wait here. I must go back for my bow."

He departed silently in the direction of the campfire and Dave's heart felt lighter.

"Good boy, Buck," he murmured encouragingly. "Stay there and don't let him down."

The dog whined a little with excitement, then gave his gruff bark once more. Dave could see the furry lump move a few inches on the limb above.

When Nequanis returned he was carrying a torch of pine

wood that burned with a bright flame. "Hold this," he told Dave. "High up, so that I can see to shoot."

As the white boy lifted the torch above his head, Nequanis bent the bow, pulling almost to his ear. The arrow flickered in the light for a split second, then buried itself in the 'coon's side. The finger-like claws let go their hold and the animal came tumbling down.

Instantly Buck was on top of the beast, clamping his powerful jaws on its throat. He held it there till the boys came up, but made no move to tear or worry it.

"Good," said Nequanis grudgingly. "Perhaps you were right. He seems to have been trained a little, after all."

They carried the dead 'coon back to camp and hung it high in a tree. It was fat and heavy. The Indian smacked his lips as he returned to the fire. "Tomorrow," he said, "we will have a feast—a raccoon stew."

They slept soundly, tired after the long day's paddling. As usual, Nequanis was up before daybreak. He skinned the 'coon and cut up the meat, stuffing the fat into a small rawhide bag which he carried among his duffel. Raccoon fat, Dave had discovered, was much prized by the Abenakis. They used it sometimes for cooking, and they rubbed their bodies with it—"to take away the man-scent while hunting," Nequanis explained. He no longer wore paint since the war party and the feast were over, and now he rubbed his face with his greasy fingers, massaging the 'coon fat into his pores.

They breakfasted on parched corn and dried venison, washed down with river water. And when Buck appeared,

AS THE WHITE BOY LIFTED THE TORCH NEQUANIS BENT THE
BOW

Dave gave him another piece of otter flesh to gnaw on.

The canoe had to be carried around the rapids. When they started paddling again the dog followed along the bank as before. By midday the stream had become narrower and the portages more frequent. They were nearly fifty miles from the Indian town now, deep in the trackless wilderness. Away to the east and south Dave could catch occasional glimpses of mountains, blue in the distance.

Shortly after noon Nequanis steered in toward the bank. "We have come far enough," he said. "Here we will hide the canoe and go southward on foot. But first you must have a lesson in shooting with the bow."

They unloaded and hauled the canoe up the bank. Turning it bottom up, they put it in a safe, dry place under low-hanging spruces. Then the Indian boy looked around until he found a level spot where he could walk off fifty paces in a straight line. Cutting a piece of birch-bark a foot square, he fastened it breast-high on a good-sized tree and went back for the bows and arrows.

Dave was surprised at the weight and stiffness of the bow in his hands. It was made from some kind of cedar, he thought. The central grip was round and nearly an inch and a half thick. Toward either end the inner surface had been cut away to a half-round and slightly tapered. Fitted to the tips were points of buck-horn, notched to hold the string.

Nequanis showed him how to string the bow, holding the lower end with his moccasin and bending the springy wood against his knee till he was able to slip the loop over the upper tip. Then he was given some practice at pulling the taut bowstring. And finally the young Indian gave him a demonstration in fitting the arrow and taking aim.

At the end of half an hour he was ready to try his hand at shooting. Nequanis led him to within twenty yards of the target and stood back out of the way.

"Shoot straight," he cautioned him. "Remember that it takes a whole day to make one good arrow."

Dave steadied the butt of the arrow between the first and second fingers of his right hand, gripping the bow and guiding the shaft with his left. He pulled back slowly and steadily, aiming at the top of the birch square. When he thought he had enough power in the bow he let fly.

The arrow wobbled a little in the air but it struck the tree six inches above the target and drove firmly into the wood.

"Too much pull," said Nequanis laconically. "And your fingers were stiff. Bring the arrow back and try again."

This time he did not bend the bow quite so far, and when he let go, his fingers slipped more smoothly off the string. The arrow went true. It cut the bark just above center.

Nequanis nodded and pointed to another spot, ten yards farther back. After an hour's practice, Dave had begun to think he was pretty good. He was hitting the target once out of four or five times, even from the fifty-yard mark.

Then the Indian boy took the bow and put four arrows in a space no bigger than the palm of his hand, shooting one after another with such apparent ease that Dave's eyes popped. All the conceit was taken out of him by that exhibition. He knew he would have to keep at it for years to equal the Indian's skill.

When they went back to their duffel, Buck was sitting beside it, on guard. The sight of him gave Nequanis an idea.

"If this dog must go with us," he said, "we will put him to work."

There were some long strips of rawhide among the supplies, and the Indian immediately set about making a sort of harness from them. In a few minutes he had put together a pack weighing twenty or thirty pounds and strapped it securely on the dog's back. Buck did not seem to mind. He shook himself once, found that the load remained in place and lay down to watch the boys prepare their own packs. When they were ready to start he got up and followed at their heels.

They went slowly, for there was no trail and Nequanis was constantly on the watch for signs of game. By sunset they were only about five miles from the river.

The Indian picked a camping place on high ground where a ledge offered a safe spot to build a fire. Dave brought dry wood and well-rotted bark for tinder, and Nequanis opened his woodchuck-skin pouch, taking out the clamshell with care. It always amazed the white boy to see a spark still alive in the slow-burning punk. Blowing on it gently, Nequanis laid it to the tinder and in a moment their fire was blazing merrily.

While Dave was cooking supper, the young Indian went out to look for water. He was gone some time, but when he returned he had good news.

"There is a spring close by," he told Dave. "I found deer tracks there and followed them. Then I came to a salt lick. We will go there before dawn and it may be we shall see a deer."

It was still pitch dark when he shook Dave awake next morning. They made no fire but took their bows and quivers of arrows and set out. The dog was left at the camping place, securely tied to a tree.

How Nequanis found his way in that inky blackness was a mystery to Dave. He thought the Indian must have owl's eyes. It wasn't until months later that he discovered the redskin's trick of feeling the path with sensitive foot soles and fingertips.

He stayed as close to his companion as he could and tried not to make any noise. When they got to the spring, Nequanis searched the ground for fresh tracks before he would let Dave drink. Then they swung to the right along a fairly well-beaten trail. That was something Dave could understand. After the animals had satisfied their craving for salt they would naturally head for the nearest water.

The boys had been moving silently along the trail for five minutes when Nequanis held out a restraining hand. Looking upward Dave saw starlight just ahead.

The lick lay in a tiny opening in the forest. It seemed to be a sort of mudhole with a crust of salt glimmering whitely around its edges. The two lads stepped off the trail into the thicker underbrush and took their stations a few feet apart, just inside the edge of the woods. Dave strung his bow and sat down silently to wait. He was cold without his blanket but he could forget that in the excitement that gripped him. Any moment now he expected to see a fine buck move out into the open glade.

The stars were growing paler now and a gray light was beginning to drive away the darkness.

They didn't have to wait long. Dave heard a faint rustle of leaves, as if the wind had stirred them. Then a low, black shape detached itself from the dark woods, not thirty feet away. Dave's heart skipped a beat as he realized it was a half-grown bear.

With trembling fingers he tried to fit his arrow to the string, but Nequanis was ahead of him. The bear snuffled with pleasure as its tongue went down to savor the salt. The next instant it gave a convulsive start, let out a high-pitched yelp of pain and turned, stumbling, toward the woods.

Nequanis whooped in triumph. He dropped his bow and sprang toward the wounded cub. With one dexterous stroke he drove his tomahawk deep into the animal's skull and it dropped to the ground in a furry mass.

Then things began to happen so fast that when he tried to remember them afterward they were only a blur in Dave's mind. There was a crashing sound back in the woods and another bear, huge and black, came charging out. It was almost on top of Nequanis before he could turn and jump back. Dave saw the young Indian launch a swinging hatchet-blow that glanced off the side of the big bear's head. Then he tripped and went down, rolling desperately to avoid those flashing teeth and ripping claws.

For a second or two Dave was paralyzed with terror. He tried to aim an arrow, but the whirling melee was too fast for his eye to follow. He could see Nequanis twisting, ducking, lunging upward with his long knife while the enraged bear snarled and struck at the moving figure with powerful forepaws.

Then a newcomer entered the fray. Dave heard a hoarse bark and a tawny streak shot out of the woods. Somehow Buck had gnawed free and raced to the rescue. In one leap the dog was at the bear's flank, sinking his teeth deep into a black haunch.

The great brute pivoted, leaving Nequanis for a moment and trying to knock Buck loose from his hold. Those few seconds gave Dave his opportunity. He pulled the bow-string back to his ear and drove the flint-tipped arrow into the bear's side just behind the shoulder.

The beast gave a gasping cough and dropped on its side, shaking its head. Nequanis had struggled to his feet. He plunged his knife into the bear's throat again and again in a kind of frenzy. Then he stood back from the dead beast and stared at the bloody shaft of Dave's arrow with blinking eyes.

He turned to the white boy. "Brother," he panted, "you have saved the life of Nequanis." And with that he slumped slowly to the ground.

Frightened, Dave rushed to his side. He could see that the Indian had lost a lot of blood. The great claws had torn away the skin and flesh for more than a foot over Nequanis' ribs. Hastily he picked the unconscious Indian up and swung him over his shoulder. Then, staggering under his burden, he hurried back to the spring.

When the cold water stung his wound, Nequanis opened his eyes and growled a protest. In a moment he was in full possession of his faculties again.

"It is not too deep," he said, looking at the ripped flesh of his side. "Leave me here and go and look for certain leaves."

He described their shape and how they grew on shrubs, in low, swampy places. Dave was lucky enough to find one of the bushes within a hundred yards of the spring. He brought back a double handful of leaves and Nequanis at once began applying them to his wound. In a few minutes the bleeding had completely stopped.

"That is medicine every Indian knows," said the young brave. "It has been kept a secret from the white men. But you are my brother. Without your arrow the old she-bear would have put me beyond the need for medicine."

He paused a little, then went on. "I was a great fool," he said simply. "Sometimes the mother bear keeps her cubs with her until she goes into a hole to sleep through the winter. I knew it but in my pride I forgot to keep watch. For that I deserve to be wounded."

There was another pause, but he still had something to

say. "The dog you call 'Buck' is a good dog," he went on at last. "He can stay with us as long as he wants."

Nequanis rested by the spring for another hour while Dave collected the weapons and made a clumsy attempt to skin the bear cub. Buck seemed to know what it was all about. He helped by pulling the hide away while the boy held the carcass.

Dave made several trips back to camp, carrying the skin and the meat. When he returned to the spring he found the young Indian standing up, holding the wet leaves against his side. His step was not quite steady but he insisted on walking back to the salt lick without Dave's help.

When he stood before the body of the big bear he made a speech.

"O strong Mother," he chanted, "my heart is heavy that this has happened to you, for I, too, am of the bear totem. Your little son I killed because my belly was hungry. You I would not have harmed except to save myself. Forgive me, Mother, and forgive my paleface brother who is without knowledge of these things."

Dave felt embarrassed by the words, but as soon as the little ritual was ended, Nequanis looked more cheerful.

"Now we will go back to the camp," he said, "and you will cook me a steak of the young bear. Tomorrow I will be strong enough to take the skin of the big one, if the wolves do not find her first."

THE WOUNDED Indian boy ate heartily of the meat Dave roasted for him, and afterward applied some of the grease to his lacerated side. Then he put fresh leaves over the injured area and lay down to sleep.

Dave could not help worrying about him. If the bleeding started again, or if the ragged flesh became infected, he was afraid his friend might die before he could get him back to the village. He kept the fire going long after dark, but when he finally rolled up in his blanket he slept soundly till daybreak.

It was just getting light when he woke suddenly and heard Buck's savage barking. It came from off in the woods near the salt lick. Hastily Dave grabbed up his bow and quiver and ran toward the sound. As he came within sight of the little glade he caught a glimpse of shadowy gray forms sneaking off into the forest. The big dog stood beside the bear's body growling fiercely, the hackles on his back and neck sticking up in an angry ridge. The bear's carcass had not been touched.

"Good work, Buck!" the boy panted. "I used to think you were part wolf, yourself, but I guess you're all dog."

He patted the big, tawny head and looked around for a target for his arrow. But the wolves had vanished.

Dave started back along the trail and was surprised to see Nequanis kneeling by the spring. The young Indian winced a little when he straightened his body, but his grin was cheerful enough.

"Look," he said, pointing at his side. "It is beginning to heal already."

And indeed Dave had to agree that the great, raw wound was doing well. A healthy-looking scab had formed over much of the torn surface. There must, he thought, be some medicinal magic in those green leaves.

They munched some dry corn for their breakfast and returned to the dead bear. Nequanis was unable to do much work, but he told Dave what to do. In the course of two or three hours the white boy had the huge skin off and was cutting away the flesh.

"Already we have made a good hunt," said Nequanis. "Not for many moons have two men of our tribe brought in more meat. Now we must start back, for most of the work will fall on you, my Brother."

Dave spent the rest of that day and most of the next packing the two skins and some two hundred pounds of meat to the river. Nequanis kept up the fire and did the cooking while his wound steadily improved. They were fortunate in having good weather—a succession of cold, clear autumn days. By the second afternoon the Indian boy was well enough to accompany Dave on his final trip, and they slept that night on the bank of the stream, close to the cached canoe.

The journey down river was slow at first. Dave had to do most of the carrying and there were half a dozen portages. He learned the trick of swinging the light birch-bark craft up to his shoulders and resting its weight on the back of his neck. Buck was a real help, for he carried a good-sized pack on each trip that the boy made.

At last, on the sixth day since leaving the Indian town, they paddled in to the landing once more. There were no crowds out to greet them, but the village dogs caught the scent of the meat and set up a tremendous barking. Then, while they were unloading, Nancy Morrison came running down the bank.

"David!" she cried. "I was worried when you were gone so long. Ooh!" She caught sight of the two bearskins. "Did *you* kill those?"

Dave laughed and reddened under his tan. "The big one, yes," he said. "Had to shoot her or she'd have made mince-meat out o' Nequanis. I'm sorry I didn't bring you a present, Nance, but we've got enough meat here to give the whole town a treat. How have you been getting on?"

"I'm all right," she said. "It's hard work but I'm going to learn how to make leggins and moccasins. Now what I do mostly is pound corn."

Looking at her more closely he saw that her face had lost some of its cheerfulness. There were lines of worry and fatigue around the mouth, but she still held her chin high.

"If they don't treat you right," he said, "tell me. Maybe I can do something to help."

Nancy saw Nequanis frowning at her and went away, leaving Dave to finish the unloading. Buck stood guard over the pile of meat, keeping the other dogs off with bared teeth until the squaws came to carry it away.

"We must go to the chief's house," Nequanis told Dave. "When a warrior has made a good hunt it is fitting that he should tell of his deeds."

Dave protested. It was all right for his Indian brother to go before the chief, but he didn't like to brag about one lucky shot. Nequanis was firm, however. He wanted Maranoquid to know that his paleface brother was a worthy member of the Abenaki tribe.

They went to their cabin and made preparations for the call. As far as Nequanis was concerned, this meant rubbing himself with grease till his body glistened, and applying some stripes of paint to his face. Dave went to the river and bathed. As he bent above the still water he thought for an instant the reflection he saw was that of an Indian. His body had taken on a tan that was only a shade lighter than the copper skin of the Abenakis.

When he returned, Nequanis looked him over with a critical eye. Something about Dave's appearance didn't satisfy him. After a moment, the Indian boy drew out his hunting knife and began whetting it carefully, first on a flat stone, then on the heel of his hand. When it was sharp enough to suit him, he approached Dave with a gleam of purpose in his eye.

Dave was alarmed. However, if he had learned one thing since his capture, it was never to show his feelings. He stood there without moving a muscle, even when Nequanis reached out suddenly and seized a handful of his hair.

"My white brother's hair is long like a woman's," said the young Indian. "If he is to be a real brave he must look like a brave."

With that he sliced off a sizable hank, close to Dave's head. The white boy felt relieved. At least he wasn't going to be scalped. His hair had grown almost to his shoulders in the last two months, and was really uncomfortable.

"Go ahead," he grinned. "Cut it all off if you like."

Methodically Nequanis went on with his barbering. Dave could only guess what was happening, but when the Indian paused for a moment he put his hand to his head and found a roach of short hair running from the crown back toward the neck.

Nequanis honed the knife again and proceeded to shave the skull on either side of the scalplock. Finally he stood back and examined the job with some pride.

"That is better," he announced. "Now my brother does not look like an owl with molting feathers. Come. We will visit the chief's house."

Some of the squaws stared and giggled as the two boys walked through the village, and Dave was having a hard time keeping his face straight when they stood at the open door of Maranoquid's lodge.

It was the largest house in the town, built of stout logs and well chinked with clay. A fine pair of moose antlers hung above the door.

A wrinkled squaw admitted them. It was dark inside, but Dave could make out the outlines of a single big room. The gray ashes of a fire lay in the center of the earth floor. Beyond them, seated on a pile of skins, was the massive figure of the chief.

He made them welcome with grave courtesy and bade them sit down on either side of him. For nearly five minutes after that not a word was spoken. Maranoquid lighted his pipe, pulled at it ceremoniously and passed it to Nequanis. The Indian boy took several slow puffs with every appearance of enjoyment. Then he rose and handed the pipe to Dave. The first mouthful of bitter smoke nearly strangled him, but by a manful effort he kept from coughing. Trying to look as placid as his host, he managed to take half a dozen small puffs before passing the rank thing back to the chief.

At length Maranoquid broke the silence. "I have smelled bear meat cooking," he said, "and the women have told me our brother, Nequanis, brought much meat home from the hunt."

"Those are true words," the young Indian replied soberly.

"We have had a good hunt, my white brother and I."

Maranoquid nodded and there was another pause while he smoked. Then he glanced at the great red wound in the young brave's side.

"I see the mark of a bear's claws on your body," he said. "I would like to hear the tale of this hunt."

"A scratch," Nequanis replied with a straight face. "But I will tell the story."

He began modestly enough, but as he warmed up to it, the yarn gained color from his vivid imagination. By the time he got to the old she-bear, Dave was squirming with embarrassment. The animal was approximately the size of a full-grown bull moose, according to Nequanis' description, and the epic struggle, knife against claw, had lasted for at least an hour.

Dave's part in the affair came in for a lesser share of glory, but even so his arrow in the bear's heart became a miracle of marksmanship—made possible, of course, by the training Nequanis had given him. No mention at all was made of Buck's brave attack on the bear. As Dave was beginning to understand, no Indian had any real appreciation of dogs.

The interview was ended at last with a series of compliments paid to both of them by the chief. They left as ceremoniously as they had entered.

Nequanis was still walking on air when they got back to their hut. He was tremendously proud of the chief's reaction to his story, and sure that he was on the way to great things.

"You heard him tell me," he bragged, "that on the next war party I will go as a full-fledged warrior and no longer as a boy? That time will come when the winter snows melt. I will carry a gun, and I will take more scalps than Bemokis —or even Cochequa!"

Dave nodded and said nothing. He admired Nequanis in some ways but there were many times when the Indian's mixture of childish vanity and cold cruelty rubbed him the wrong way.

As soon as he had a chance he went off by himself to the river bank and looked at his reflection in the water. It made him shudder to realize how much like a redskin he had become. Except for the lighter color of his scalplock he would have been shot at for an Indian in any white settlement.

. . . .

Nequanis' side healed quickly, thanks to his own medicine and the mysterious messes brewed by the M'teoulin. In less than a week he was ready to go on another hunt.

Dave, meanwhile, had practiced with the bow every day and made a steady improvement in his shooting. It was a proud moment for him when he finally brought down a gray squirrel from the upper branches of an oak tree. After that Nequanis showed him how to throw the tomahawk, and he spent hours flipping the light hatchet at a mark ten paces off. In the secret plan that was already firmly fixed in his head, all these accomplishments would be useful.

A three-day September storm came on the day when they had planned to start on their hunt. It beat down

DAVE LOOKED AT HIS REFLECTION IN THE WATER

fiercely from the north, stripping the leaves from many of the trees and driving the smoke of the fires back into the lodges.

When Dave could stand the choking smudge in the cabin no longer, he wrapped his blanket around him and sallied out to see if he could find Nancy Morrison.

He located her at last in the house of Bemokis. The bent-backed warrior himself had gone to a council in the chief's lodge, but two or three Indian women were squatting on the floor and Nancy was among them. The girl had a deerskin in her hands and was chewing valiantly on a large mouthful of it.

The squaws scowled and said nothing, but he went in anyway.

"Gosh, Nancy!" he exclaimed. "What are you doing that for? You aren't that hungry, are you?"

She hauled the limp hide out of her mouth and laughed.

"Of course not," she said. "This is the way all the best skins have to be fixed. It keeps them soft. But my jaws do get pretty tired."

Dave's nose wrinkled in disgust. "It must be nasty-tasting stuff," he answered. "It's a shame they make you do such things."

Nancy chuckled. "Don't you worry about me," she said. "This is a lot easier than hoeing or pounding corn meal. Besides they haven't cut *my* hair off and made me look like a skinned rabbit!"

She tossed her yellow curls. "You'd better not stay in

here," she added. "They don't like prisoners to see much of each other."

"All right," Dave replied sulkily, "I'll get out. But I wanted to make sure you were being treated right. You won't see me for a while anyway. We're going hunting again as soon as the rain stops."

The saucy look went out of her eyes at once. "Take care of yourself, David," she said quietly. "Don't get in any more fights with bears. I'll be looking for you when you come back."

Girls were queer creatures, he thought, as he stumbled back through the rain. One minute they were imps and the next they were sweet as pie.

He spent the rest of the day fitting a new shaft to a broken arrow and sharpening his knife and tomahawk. The big dog, Buck, had been allowed inside the lodge during the storm and he watched Dave's movements with alert interest. When preparations like these were being made, he knew there was going to be another hunt. And his bushy tail drummed softly on the clay floor at the prospect.

<h1 style="text-align:center">XIV</h1>

THERE was a heavy, white frost on the ground the morning they started. Dave half expected to see ice rimming the streams, but Nequanis assured him another moon would pass before the river froze.

As before, Buck kept pace with their canoe, ranging along the bank, but this time he was not afraid to show himself in the open.

There was a larger hunting party in three canoes a few miles behind them. Nequanis had made an early start in order to keep in the lead if possible. Nevertheless he stayed close to the bank most of the day, searching for signs of game. The other Indians did not overtake them. Just at dusk they heard two or three gunshots, very faint, from downstream.

"They have found something," Nequanis grumbled. "Perhaps we should have seen it, but that dog of yours frightened it away."

"That may be true," Dave admitted, "but my brother knows that the deer do not come down to drink in daylight. Look—" his voice sank to a whisper—"there—straight ahead!"

A hundred yards up the river a two-point buck was tiptoeing daintily down the bank. Without a sound, Nequanis swung the canoe in to the shore and tied it. Motioning to Dave to stay where he was, the Indian climbed the bank and vanished in the woods.

The white boy held his breath and waited. He could see the deer's great ears twitch nervously and its nose move from side to side, testing the light breeze for hostile scents. Then the antlered head went down quickly as the buck drank.

There was no sound from the woods, and Dave had to guess at the young brave's progress. He was sure Nequanis could not have made more than half the distance when he saw the buck's head jerk erect. With a snort, it spun about, stood for a second or two listening, then made a graceful leap that carried it to the top of the bank. At that instant an arrow swished out of nowhere and drove into the deer's neck. Dave heard his friend's triumphant yell and knew he no longer had to stay in the canoe.

He seized his bow and jumped ashore, running through the forest toward the place where the buck had disappeared. A yellow-brown flash went past him before he had taken a dozen strides. Buck was chasing the wounded deer.

Nequanis was gone by the time Dave reached the animal's

drinking place, but he could follow the hunt by ear. There was a crashing among the trees and a brief yelp of pain from the dog. Afterward he heard the Indian boy shout again exultantly. Running toward the sounds, he came on Nequanis standing over the dead buck, his bloody knife lifted high. Buck was licking a hoof-slash in his side.

In boasting about the kill, Nequanis said little about the dog's help, but Dave could see that the arrow had not inflicted a fatal wound. The tendon in one of the deer's hind legs had been cut by sharp teeth and powerful jaws. Then the Indian had come up to finish the animal off.

Between them they dragged the two-hundred-pound buck out to the river bank.

"We can camp here," said Nequanis. "You go and bring up the canoe while I skin the deer."

He had the hide off by the time Dave had unloaded the duffel and built a fire. They feasted on liver that night. Nequanis made a big bundle of the rest of the meat, and wrapped it up in the skin with a birch pole through the middle for easier carrying.

They rose in the dark next morning, for the young Indian wanted to keep well ahead of the other party. He was careful, however, to leave the buck's hoofs and horns beside the ashes of their fire, so that the warriors who followed would be sure to see them.

Before the frost was melted by the sun, Nequanis picked up another deer track a few miles above their camping place. They hid the canoe in a fir thicket, hung the meat in a tree and followed the trail with light packs on their backs.

This was hard work, Dave discovered. The tracks were easy to follow for the first hour. After that the frost was gone and it became a task for an expert tracker. Nequanis moved along through the rough brush, his knees bent and his sharp eyes searching every fallen leaf and bit of earth. Dave had all he wanted to do just to keep up with him. However, he was beginning to use his own eyes in studying the trail. He could already tell a buck track from that of a doe by its size, depth and the blunt, splayed toes that came from pawing the earth. Now he found that a traveling deer left very few recognizable tracks on dry ground. The young Indian had to follow by other signs. A twisted leaf, or a green twig bent ever so little from its normal direction, seemed to give him all the information he needed.

They held to the trail for three or four hours before Nequanis took time for a rest. The deer had stopped to feed here, he said, so he didn't think it knew any enemy was following. It was a big doe, and it was moving in zigzags from one feeding place to another rather than in a straight line.

They chewed a few kernels of corn and pushed on. Both of them were tired when they stopped again an hour past noon.

"She has not caught our scent yet," said Nequanis, "but she is afraid of something. She travels up-wind. We have come far and we must kill soon or go back to the river. You stay here and keep the dog quiet. I will go faster alone."

166

BEFORE HE HAD TIME TO GROW SHAKY THE DOE CAME OUT
OF THE WOODS

Dave looked about for Buck but couldn't find him. He had kept them company all morning but he was gone now.

As soon as Nequanis was out of sight, Dave hid himself in a clump of spruce and settled down to wait. He knew you could never tell when game might appear, so he strung his bow and laid an arrow close to his hand. Not more than twenty minutes had passed when he heard Buck's bark. It was a long way off at first but it came nearer moment by moment. The dog was running—chasing something straight toward Dave's thicket.

With sudden excitement, the boy rose to one knee and fitted the arrow to his bowstring. Then, before he had time to grow shaky, the doe came out of the woods. She was running blindly, tongue out, and coming almost directly at him. He aimed for her heaving chest and let the arrow go. There was no time to see whether he had hit the mark, for the deer was almost on top of him. He ducked and rolled out of the way as she plowed into the thicket.

When he regained his feet he could see the big reddish-gray body on its side, thrashing about in the brush a few yards away. He drew his long-bladed knife and approached the wounded deer cautiously, trying to keep clear of those flailing, spear-sharp hoofs. Then she rolled over on her knees and he saw his chance.

Before the doe could rise he landed on her neck and shoulders and jerked the knife upward into her throat. The great gush of blood sickened him, and his knees were shaking as he stepped aside. He knew then that killing would never be easy for him, even when it must be done.

The doe died where she lay. Wearily Dave crawled out of the thicket and found Buck sitting on his haunches, his strong teeth gleaming in a wide grin. He patted the big dog approvingly.

"You're quite a fellow, Buck," he told him. "Where'd you learn that trick of heading off the game and driving it back, huh? Maybe you thought it up yourself. Mighty smart dog!"

There seemed to be no point in shouting for Nequanis. The Indian must have heard Buck's barking and given up the hunt in disgust. He would be back before long, Dave thought.

He sat down to wait. The minutes dragged into hours and still Nequanis didn't return. Finally Dave nodded off to sleep.

A hand shaking his shoulder woke him with a start. The tall Indian boy stood beside him, his shoulders stooped and eyes hollow with fatigue.

"Get up, lazy one," Nequanis said. "Build a fire. It is near sunset and we must camp where we are."

"I—I thought you'd be back when you heard the dog," Dave replied. "What happened?"

"I killed the doe," said the young brave, "but it was far from here."

"*You* killed the doe!" cried Dave in astonishment. "Look —there she is in that clump of spruce. Buck drove her straight to me and I shot her."

Nequanis stared. "Then there must have been two," he said in puzzlement. "Mine was the doe we were trailing. Let me look at yours."

A smile of delight overspread his tired face as he peered into the thicket. "You have done well, Brother," he said. "Two fine deer in a single day! The men of the tribe will say we are good hunters, you and I."

Nequanis had skinned his doe and cached the meat, which was one reason he had been so long. Now, as soon as the fire was going, he showed Dave how to take the hide off the second deer. The white boy was clumsy but eager to learn. They ate the liver and tongue for supper and gave Buck all he could hold of the less desirable parts. The meat and the skin they hoisted into a tree fork for safe keeping.

There was another hard frost that night and they would have been cold in their blankets if Buck hadn't curled his furry bulk close between them. Even Nequanis was forced to admit that the dog was more of a help than a nuisance.

In the morning they tramped through the woods to the place where the Indian had shot the deer.

As they approached the spot, a grayish animal dropped out of a tree ahead and went bounding off into the brush. Nequanis gave an exclamation of disgust, then went forward at a run.

The bundle of venison had been pulled part way out of the crotch where he had placed it, and some of the meat was torn. It hung in shreds from the end of the deerskin wrapping.

"A lynx!" said the Indian. "If we had been only a little slower, that robber would have taken it all."

They divided the meat into two packs and carried it back to their camp. Buck had been left there on guard, and the venison from Dave's doe was undisturbed. It took two trips to transport all the meat to the river, but they made it before dark. And next morning they loaded the meat and skins of all three deer into the canoe and started for home.

.   .   .   .

They went on other hunts that fall but none turned out as successfully as the first two. Dave had begun to think killing game was easy. He learned by hard experience that luck, weather and the unpredictable habits of animals made it far more difficult than he had supposed.

Once they were overtaken by a sudden early snowfall deep in the wilderness. They went to sleep one night and woke at dawn to find themselves buried under a foot of fluffy white. Without snowshoes they were unable to follow the game, although tracks of deer were plentiful.

On another trip they tramped through many miles of forest and never saw so much as a squirrel or a partridge. All night long the wolves howled, and they caught one or two glimpses of lean, gray wolf-shadows stealing through the woods. But it seemed that every other animal had fled the country or gone into hiding.

The heavy work toughened Dave and taught him how to keep alive in the forest, even though they had little to show for their efforts. He had grown an inch or two since he left home. His muscles were hard and his senses keen. In everything but the color of his eyes and hair and the thoughts in his head, he was as much an Indian as Nequanis. He had even taken to greasing his body when he found it helped keep him warm on the trail.

It was hard for him to keep track of the calendar, but as nearly as he could reckon, it was mid-November when the Canadian winter shut down in earnest. There was a pale ring around the moon one night. The medicine man saw it and began beating on the drum. When the warriors and their squaws were gathered around him, he performed a few acts of magic, mumbled two or three incantations and let out one of his sudden yells.

At last he told them that he had been talking to the spirits. In two days, he said, there would be much snow and cold. If his hearers knew what was good for them they would quickly put leaves and branches around the sills of their lodges to keep out the wind. The squaws would gather plenty of wood and the braves would cut rawhide and put fresh webbing in their snowshoes.

Dave was surprised that they didn't laugh in the old man's face, for that ring around the moon must have told its own story to every weather-wise Indian in the village. But they thanked him gravely and went back to their houses. For all his silly antics they must have some superstitious fear of his powers, the boy thought.

The town was actually in pretty good shape for winter. The corn and pumpkins had long since been harvested.

From the Co-hos intervales, far away on the Connecticut, the work party had brought in three canoe-loads of food the month before. And all through the autumn the squaws had been smoking meat and drying fish.

All these provisions were kept in a common storehouse next to the chief's lodge. There were no locks on it, but a dog was tied at each of the corners to keep away rats and weasels. Any family in need of food could go there and take what was wanted as long as the supplies held out.

It was hard for Dave to believe that nobody would cheat under such a system. When he asked Nequanis about it, he learned that any Indian who stole food he did not need would be banished from the tribe forever.

"We Abenakis are used to having lean stomachs in the winter," the young brave explained. "There is no feasting, except when some hunter brings in fresh meat. Nobody eats more than he has to, for all of us know the food must last until the time of flying birds."

Matawassie had gone to live with another of the younger braves after his quarrel with Nequanis, so Dave and his Indian brother had the cabin to themselves. They banked it with spruce boughs and chinked the cracks with clay from the river bank. Then, with enough wood for a week's fires piled under the eaves and a stock of corn and jerked meat laid by, they were ready for the weather to do its worst.

XV

THE STORM began in the night and snow fell steadily for forty-eight hours. With it came a drop in temperature and a biting wind that wailed around the log walls and drove dry snow through chinks no wider than a hair.

The boys paid little attention to the weather for they were busy. First Nequanis took down his snowshoes from the pole rafters and tested the thongs. They were fairly tight, but he found several frayed strands of rawhide that needed replacing. When that job was done, he started making a new pair for Dave.

Outside, on a rack, half a dozen long strips of cedar wood had been seasoning for months. The Indian chose four pieces about seven feet long and brought them inside. He trimmed them evenly with his knife, then took a pair and set two braces of spruce between them, about fifteen inches apart. He told Dave to bend the tips together while he did the same thing at the opposite end.

The tough, springy wood curved under their grip. As soon as Nequanis had his two ends together, he whipped a deerskin thong securely around them, then bound the tips Dave held in similar fashion. The result was a long, canoe-shaped frame, over six feet in length and a little less than a foot wide.

When the other frame was put together, the Indian began cutting long, narrow strips from a piece of thin-scraped moose hide. It took many yards of these thongs to weave the filling for a pair of snowshoes, and the two boys worked at it most of the day. By evening they had the thongs all cut, but there was one other job to be done before they could start stringing.

They put a huge kettle of snow over the fire, melted it and brought the water to a furious boil. Then Nequanis put the front end of one snowshoe frame into the pot and laid a cover over it so that the wood was bathed in steam. When he took it out after a few minutes, the cedar had softened enough to be bent. He thrust the tip into a chink between two logs, a foot above the ground, and the weight of the frame brought the other end down to the floor. As Dave could see, this operation put a slight curl in the toe of the shoe.

The Indian left it there to stiffen and went through the same procedure with the other frame. Then they lay down to sleep.

The wind went down in the night but the snow kept on

falling. Again they stayed indoors, tying the thongs to the snowshoe frames, stretching them tight and knotting the web together in the approved Abenaki way.

"Now," said Nequanis at last, "you have a good pair of snowshoes. You can go with me across the deepest drifts, and there will be some that are deeper than a tall man's head. The storm will be over tomorrow and I will show you how."

Sure enough, the snow stopped about the time it grew dark, and a still, biting cold followed. Huddled in his blanket, Dave slept close to the embers of the fire that night. In the morning, even inside the cabin, the steam of his breath froze in his nostrils.

Nequanis had a sort of loose deerskin jacket with the hair inside, and he put it on while Dave built up the fire. When he opened the flimsy door, a breast-high wall of snow shut out the light.

Dave looked around helplessly for a shovel, but the Indian boy knew how to clear the doorway. He took one of his snowshoes in both hands and dug away the white, fluffy mass without difficulty. In a few moments he had made a three-foot path, sloping upward to the top of the drifts, and another short tunnel to the woodpile under the eaves.

When the task was finished they slipped their moccasins into the broad loops of the snowshoes and sallied out, Dave shivering in his blanket.

"We will see if the squaws can make you one of these," said Nequanis, pointing to his deerskin coat. "A true warrior could go naked through the forest on such a day as this, but you still have some of the white man's softness."

Dave might have asked why Nequanis wore the jacket, but his teeth were chattering too much for easy conversation.

He learned the art of walking on the long shoes quickly enough. After tripping himself once and scuffing his ankles a few times, he caught the knack of keeping his knees farther apart than in a normal stride. The web bore him up beautifully, so that he sank only a few inches into a six-foot drift of snow.

Smoke was coming from the roof-holes of the lodges and there was a smell of cooking food in the air. Through most of the winter season the Indians kept a pot of corn meal mush near the fire, flavoring it with scraps of bear fat, jerked venison, dried berries and any other tidbits they happened to have. Dave didn't mind the taste of it, but it sometimes grew monotonous. More than once he dreamed at night of his mother's hot biscuits, dripping with butter and maple syrup, or her spicy, brown-crusted apple pies.

They stopped in front of the house of Bemokis, and it was the bent-backed brave himself who spoke from the shadows, bidding them enter. There was a good fire inside and it was warm.

Bemokis' evil face scowled at the sight of the white boy. "The food is ready," he said gruffly and motioned to the kettle.

They accepted the invitation, such as it was, and squatted

down, dipping their fingers into the hot mush. As he ate, Dave looked about between mouthfuls, wondering where his little friend Nancy might be. A sound of whispering and giggling came from behind a curtain of skins and he remembered that the squaws kept out of sight when their lord and master had visitors.

There was no talk until the boys and their host had filled their stomachs. Then Nequanis belched politely and began the conversation. For several minutes he and Bemokis discussed the weather and the prospects of finding game in the deep snow. Finally the Indian boy got around to the point.

"My white brother feels the cold," he remarked, "for he has no coat of skins. Perhaps Bemokis may have such a garment—an old one, no longer worn, which he has not thrown away."

The older Indian grunted. "That may be," he replied. "But as it happens, the white girl prisoner has already begun sewing skins to make a coat for him."

He turned toward the curtain. "Come out, small one with hair the color of corn," he commanded.

Nancy must have been waiting for the summons, for she appeared instantly. She was smiling with delight, and her proud hands held up a fine new deerskin jacket, complete to the last stitch.

"Gosh!" Dave breathed. "For me? And all finished?"

She nodded. "Motaqua showed me how. She's Bemokis' wife. And I've been sewing ever since the snow started. Here—see if it's big enough."

He dropped his blanket and slipped his bare arms into the roomy sleeves. The soft hair felt warm and comfortable against his skin. Pulling the coat about him, he tied the cord at the waist and turned slowly before the admiring eyes of Nancy and Nequanis.

"It's wonderful, Nance," he beamed. "You're a mighty smart girl. I sure will have to bring you something special, next time I go hunting."

The boys went back to their cabin to leave Dave's blanket, and found the big dog, Buck, sitting in the doorway. He had curled up outside the log wall after the snow began and slept there comfortably until the end of the storm. The heat of his body had made a neat, round cavern, deep under the drifts, and they could see it by peering into the hole through which he had crawled out. They fed him, banked the fire in the hut, and went off to the woods.

Nequanis suggested that Dave carry an ax. "You can cut wood for the fire while I set some snares," he said.

They tramped a mile or more into the forest. When they came to a hollow above a small, frozen stream, the Indian lad scooped away some of the snow and began constructing a snare close to the bank. He pulled down the top of a limber birch sapling, fastened one end of a loop of deer sinew to it, and held it down with two braced sticks, so delicately set that a light touch would loosen them and let the tree spring straight.

Dave attempted to make one of his own, and after a few tries he succeeded in setting a snare farther up the stream.

He wasn't exactly sure what he might catch in it, but Nequanis told him mink and even otter were sometimes trapped this way. When the Indian had prepared half a dozen snares they went back, cutting wood and carrying bundles of fagots home with them.

Dave found that as long as he was moving, the skin coat kept him warm. It had a sort of hood that came up over his shaved head but there were no pockets. As a consequence his hands were almost numb with cold, and he wished many times for the knitted wool mittens his mother used to make for him.

One day was very like another in the snowbound Indian town. Most of the older warriors lay in their lodges, ate, slept and smoked pipes with their friends. The women trudged out on snowshoes to gather wood or set snares for rabbits. Only the younger and more adventurous braves took the hunting trail in such weather.

Dave and Nequanis visited their traps each day but for a week they caught nothing but one skinny rabbit. This the Indian gave to Buck, who gobbled it down in half a dozen mouthfuls. Rabbit fur was good winter food for dogs, Nequanis said. It made their own fur come in thicker, or at least such was the Abenaki belief.

On the seventh day after the big storm, it snowed again lightly on top of the crust, and the young Indian announced that they would go hunting as soon as it stopped. Next morning they took two days' rations and their bows and quivers and set out northwestward across the frozen river.

"I had a dream last night," Nequanis said. "My manitou —my familiar spirit—told me we would find meat if we took this trail. It is barren country and our hunters do not often go this way, but my manitou knows the minds of animals. See—in this new snow it is easy to follow tracks."

The tracks were plain enough, but the only ones they saw in half a day's plodding were the prints of snowshoe rabbits, woodmice, squirrels and jays. They went on through the short winter afternoon and just before sunset Nequanis stopped, a whispered exclamation on his lips. He pointed to a hollow in the snow a dozen feet ahead.

Dave stared without comprehending. "A big animal," breathed the Indian. "Perhaps a moose. Come quietly."

There was another hollow a few feet beyond the first— then another and another. The white boy began to understand. Some heavy beast had wallowed along through the deep drifts, making a succession of leaps, but that must have been before the new snow fell.

Nequanis was running now, and Dave had trouble keeping close to him. Just as the red ball of the sun went below the horizon he heard the long quavering howl of a wolf. It was hard to tell where it came from, but it seemed to spur Nequanis on. He hurried forward in long strides, the tails of his snowshoes flicking little puffs of snow behind him.

Dave saw the other boy pull an arrow out of the quiver and pause long enough to string his bow. Not knowing what to expect, he did the same thing. Then they raced on once more, still following the half-obliterated trail. They had gone perhaps five hundred yards when they heard the wolf cry again, close at hand and broken, as if by the sound of panting.

Nequanis slowed his step and went forward more cautiously. In the dusk ahead Dave saw something move but couldn't tell what it was. The Indian boy fitted his arrow to the cord. He took three or four more strides, then set himself for the shot.

The twang of the bowstring was followed by a coughing yelp of pain. Some thirty yards away Dave saw a big grayish-white timber wolf jump straight up into the air and fall back floundering in the snow. He expected Nequanis to rush in and finish the brute with his hatchet, but the Indian boy advanced warily, holding another arrow ready in his hand.

Dave understood why when he caught a glimpse of a second wolf sneaking away among the trees. The animal Nequanis had shot appeared to be dead when they reached it, but the young brave made sure with a blow of his tomahawk.

."Now," he whispered, "the moose!"

The words made little sense to Dave until he remembered those sunken depressions in the snow. The wolves had been hunting the same quarry as themselves!

The two boys pushed on eagerly for another hundred yards. It was growing darker every moment. Suddenly Nequanis stopped and clutched Dave's arm. Peering in the direction his finger pointed, Dave made out a big, dark shape against the snow. It was the head and antlers of a bull moose, buried shoulder-deep in a drift!

As they watched, the animal gave a great bound that carried it forward a few feet. It was a mighty effort but it did little good, for the next second the moose was as deep in the snow as before.

Nequanis uttered a wild yell of joy and dashed forward, but Dave stayed where he was. There was no pleasure for him in this kind of hunting. Something about the huge beast's struggles made him sick at heart, and he turned his eyes away until it was over.

When he approached, the moose was dead. Nequanis had driven an arrow into its brain, just behind the eye. Dave stood staring, for this was the biggest animal he had ever seen. The immense head and the six-foot spread of horns made him think of some fabulous monster out of a fairy tale.

The Indian boy regarded his prize with satisfaction. "There will be no fat on this one," he said, "for he was very tired. The wolves would have killed him if we had not been here. But he is a very big moose. His hide and such meat as he has on him will make us heroes in the village. Now we must build a fire and a shelter, for soon it will be night and the wolves will come back."

With a snowshoe he dug out a space in the snow a few yards from the body of the moose. It was a sort of room with walls of white, five or six feet high on three sides, and the trunk of a big spruce on the other. The thick, overhanging boughs of the tree made a roof.

184

THE ANIMAL GAVE A GREAT BOUND THAT CARRIED IT FOR-
WARD A FEW FEET

Dave brought wood and tinder and they soon had a bright blaze going in a hollow between two roots. With its light to guide them they dug a tunnel out into the drift and uncovered the body of the moose. It was already stiffening and Nequanis urged as much speed as possible, for they must get the skin off before the carcass froze.

When they had enough clear space to work in, they set to at once. In half an hour the huge hide was stripped off. As Nequanis had foretold, the moose was gaunt almost to the point of emaciation, but there were still many pounds of tough, stringy meat on its great frame.

Dave looked at the pile of flesh they cut off with some misgiving. "How are we ever going to carry all this home?" he asked. "And the hide, too. That must weigh fifty pounds."

Nequanis grinned. "You will see tomorrow," he promised. "It will be easier than you think. But we must be on guard all night and keep the fire burning. One of us will sleep while the other watches. You, my Brother, can have the first sleep, as soon as we have eaten."

XVI

THEY made a good meal of moose liver, and Dave curled up in a bed of spruce boughs, spread on the ground. The warmth of the fire was reflected by the walls of snow, and he was so comfortable that he fell asleep at once. It seemed to him that he had hardly closed his eyes when Nequanis was shaking him awake.

"Keep the fire bright," said the Indian. "The wolves are near, for I have heard their voices. But they will not come too close to a flame. Wake me when it begins to grow light."

The five or six hours Dave spent on guard were uneasy ones. He tried not to drowse off, for the fire had to be fed with sticks every few minutes. Once, when he went out to gather more wood, he saw a pair of glowing eyes in the brush close by. And at intervals the wolves howled eerily, far and near.

When the first gray came into the sky he roused Nequanis. There was more fresh meat for breakfast, and as soon as they had finished their meal they prepared to start for home.

Dave was still curious to see how the Indian intended to carry their booty. The hide had been left flat on the bottom of the tunnel and was now frozen almost as stiff as a board. Nequanis hacked away two long, narrow strips from its sides, where the cut had been made down the belly. The ends of these he tied firmly through slits in the hindquarters of the skin. Then he piled the frozen meat, piece after piece, in the middle of the hide. There must have been nearly three hundred pounds of it.

"It is what the Algonquins call a 'toboggan,' " he said. "Now we go."

He handed Dave one of the rawhide strips and he took the other. To the white boy's surprise, the load pulled easily over the snow. The stiff hide made a serviceable sled, and its broad, flat surface rode over the tops of the drifts without sinking in.

They stopped where Nequanis had killed the wolf, but there was only a bloody patch in the snow and a maze of deep tracks to show where it had been. The beast's cannibal brothers had disposed of the body in the night.

Before dark the boys reached the river and crossed on the snow-covered ice. The lodges were dark and silent in the twilight and only the smell of wood smoke and one or two faintly glowing windows showed that it was inhabited.

Nequanis gave a great shout as the two tired boys gained the top of the river bank. The dogs began barking and heads popped out of doorways.

"Moose!" cried the young Indian. "Meat for a feast and for the storehouse. Come and get it!"

Almost instantly squaws wrapped in blankets came waddling forth from the cabins on their snowshoes. There were shrieks of joy and high-pitched chants of praise for the young hunters. Dave and Nequanis turned the meat over to the women and went to their own hut, where Buck was waiting for them.

There was a feast that night in the chief's house, and afterward the usual ceremony in which Nequanis was called upon to tell the story of the hunt. Dave sat uncomfortably through the boastful account. At least his own name did not enter too much into the tale, for he had contributed little to the killing of the moose.

It was after midnight when they got to bed, and both boys slept late next morning. As they were eating breakfast, Dave made some inquiry about the habits of moose. It seemed strange to him that so powerful an animal should be so helpless in the winter drifts.

Nequanis told him that when the Great Spirit made the animals, each was given protection against its enemies. "He gave long legs to the moose," said the Indian boy. "He measured the snow after a deep fall, and said, 'Moose is too heavy to walk on the crust. I will give him the longest legs of any animal, so that his belly will be as high as a man's shoulders.' And so it was done.

"But," said Nequanis, "the Great Spirit had forgotten Wuchowsen, the Wind Blower. When the snow lies flat, the moose wades through it without trouble. But sometimes Wuchowsen beats his wings and blows the snow into great drifts. Then, if the moose is wise, he stays in one place, where he has trampled out a yard for himself. If he tries to travel he may be caught, as this one was, in drifts too deep even for his long legs."

They went out, that day, to visit their snares. Dave was alone when he approached the one he had set, and his heart gave a jump when he saw that the sapling was no longer bent in a curve but standing almost straight. Then, in his excitement, he shouted to Nequanis. For up there above his head hung a long, furry body, almost jet black in color.

The Indian boy came on the run. His mouth opened in astonishment at the sight of the catch.

"A fisher!" he exclaimed. "You are very lucky, Brother. In all the years I have trapped, this is the first one I ever saw caught in a snare."

Dave pulled down the sapling and took the stiff body out of the deer-sinew noose. The animal was long and slim, like a mink, only three or four times as large. Its fur was soft, deep and glossy.

"That skin is worth three beaver," Nequanis told him. "It would make a warm lining for the winter hood of a chief's daughter."

Dave nodded. He had his own ideas about what to do with his prize. The boys skinned the fisher that afternoon and stretched the pelt over a slab of wood whittled to the proper shape. The next morning the white boy took it with him and went to the lodge of Bemokis. Nancy came to the door.

"The head of the house is not at home," she told him saucily in Abenaki. "And it is not proper for young braves to enter where the squaws are."

She giggled. "Really, I'm not allowed to let you in, Dave," she said. "But I'm glad to see you wearing the jacket. It's nice, even if I do say so myself."

"Sure is," Dave grinned. "It kept me fine and warm on that hunt. Remember I promised to bring you a present? Here it is. Like it?"

She took the fisher pelt, and her eyes grew big as saucers.

"O-o-oh!" she gasped. "It's lovely! You caught it yourself, Dave—for me?"

Before he could move she threw both arms around his neck and kissed him. Then she whisked into the house and the door was closed after her.

"Thank you, David!" he heard her call from inside.

Dave looked around hastily to make sure none of the braves had seen what happened. Then, pulling the hood over his head to hide his crimson face, he went crunching off on his snowshoes. It was half an hour before he dared go back to his cabin.

．　　．　　．　　．　　．　　．　　．

Back in New England, Dave had thought he was used to long winters, but this Canadian winter seemed to have no end. The short, gray days offered little chance for adventure or change. The boys tended their trapline, practiced with

NEQUANIS DROPPED HIS WEIGHTED LINE THROUGH THE HOLE

the bow or mended their equipment. Sometimes, between blizzards, they made brief hunting trips, but they found no more helpless moose waiting to be killed.

Food began to run low in the storehouse before February was over, and they ate their corn sparingly, saving every dry kernel. Chief Maranoquid held a council, at which he said a band of the older and more experienced hunters would go up the river and try to find a winter yard of deer or moose. At the same time he urged the young braves to snare small game and catch fish through the ice.

Ice-fishing was new to Dave. He helped Nequanis dig snow for an hour to get down to the river's surface. Then they went to work with their axes, hacking into the ice. It was two feet thick and hard as glass, but they finally succeeded in cutting a hole a foot in diameter and came to black water that welled up from its bottom.

With numb fingers Nequanis baited a hook with a precious shred of jerked venison and dropped his weighted line through the hole. Then he squatted on his heels to wait. Dave stood it for a few minutes, but he soon found himself shaking with the cold. He rose, moving his feet and thrashing his arms.

Nequanis frowned. "My white brother is too soft," he whispered. "The fish will be frightened if you move and make noises. If you cannot wait quietly as I do, go to the village and sit in a warm lodge like the women."

Dave climbed out on the bank and ran up and down to get his blood circulating. When he came back, the Indian boy was still hunched in the same spot, motionless except for an occasional jiggle of the line. Dave had been watching for several minutes and was beginning to feel the cold again when he saw Nequanis give the line a quick jerk. Then he jumped to his feet and began pulling with might and main. And at last he hauled a huge, wriggling eel up through the hole. It was nearly three feet long and as big around as his wrist.

The young Indian uttered no word, but his grin showed that he was pleased. With patient fingers he extracted the hook and rebaited it. This time he used a sliver cut from the eel itself. He dropped it through the ice and in five seconds was dragging in another catch as big as the first. This was the kind of action Dave, too, could enjoy. He hurried down to join his friend and helped by cutting more strips of bait.

The flurry of bites lasted several minutes, then stopped as suddenly as it had begun. But there were eight fat eels on the ice when it was over, and eel meat was cooking in every pot in the village that night.

Dave had seen Father Pierre quite often that winter. The priest had his own snowshoes and stalked about the town in his black robes, paying pastoral calls on his copper-skinned parishioners. Several times the white boy had gone to chapel on Sunday mornings. It was after one of these services that Father Pierre stopped him at the door of the little church. The priest reminded him that he had not yet called at his house.

"There is somet'ing I weesh to tell you," he said. "You weel see w'en you come."

Dave felt sorry for the gaunt, sad-faced man of God. Having nothing else to do that afternoon, he knocked at Father Pierre's door and was welcomed inside.

After months of living in Indian lodges, the interior of the little house gave him a sudden pang of homesickness. It was simple and bare, but very clean. There were no pictures on the whitewashed walls, but a crucifix hung opposite the door. A polished deal table occupied the center of the room, and two chairs were placed beside it. In one corner was a narrow cot and in another a beautifully carved chest of drawers, obviously brought from France.

The priest must have seen the look of pleasure in Dave's eyes.

"You lak', eh?" he said in his labored English. "Eet mak' you weesh for 'ome, no?"

Dave nodded. "I speak Abenaki," he replied in the dialect. "Perhaps we can understand each other better if we talk in the Indian tongue. These things you have here— yes, they are beautiful. And as you say, they make me wish for home."

Father Pierre looked at him questioningly. "You are not all Indian, then," he said, "even though you dress in the Abenaki fashion. I have heard that you make progress with the bow and the tomahawk, and are on the way to becoming a skillful hunter."

He closed his eyes and seemed to meditate before he

went on.

"Even though you are not of my faith," he said with a tired smile, "there is something in my heart that goes out to you. It is hard for me to watch a civilized boy turn into a savage."

He wrung his thin hands unhappily. "There are those in the high command at Quebec who would not agree with me, but"—he shrugged—"they are a long way off."

Slowly he turned and went to the carved chest. "Come," he said. "I have something to show you."

Dave watched him as he unlocked the top drawer with a brass key. Out of it he took a folded paper that crackled as he spread it out on the table. It was a map, laboriously drawn by an unskilled hand. There had been many erasures, and the paper was stained and torn.

"This is the work of many years," said the priest. "I was a young man when I came to the River of the Wolves. Many times I went with the hunters to the east and the south. Also I talked with old men of the tribe who had crossed the Height of Land in the days when the English drove the Abenaki from their hunting grounds and they fled to Canada.

"Much of the country I have drawn I saw with my own eyes—traveled over it on my own feet or by canoe. You, too, went up the river before the snow fell. How far did you go?"

"Three days," Dave answered, wondering. "We went till there was only a little water and many carries."

Father Pierre nodded. "I know that place. See—here it

is on the map. If you had gone half a day farther you would have come to a little lake among high hills. That is the source of the river, and that is as far as most of the Indians have ever gone. They believe that devils live in the hills above."

He paused, his eyes on some far-off place, and Dave waited.

"But," said the priest, coming back to the map, "I climbed those hills. And from the summit I could see many leagues to the southward. It was a wild, rough country, but close to the foot of the hills a chain of lakes began."

His finger traced their pattern on the map. "The largest lake," he said, "is called Ourangabena, and the stream that flows from it to the south has a French name—the Little St. François. Follow that river and what do you see?"

Dave bent over the map. He saw where the St. François, after a winding course of many miles, joined a much bigger river. Its name was neatly written down—*Rivière St. Jean.*

For a moment the words meant nothing to the boy. Then some memory clicked in his brain. *Jean* was the same as *John* in English. The St. John River! He had heard sailors tell of the big river far to the east, beyond the province of Maine. It came from somewhere up in Canada and flowed south into the Bay of Fundy.

Dave looked up, a startled question in his eyes. Was he mistaken in thinking the priest gave a little nod in reply?

Father Pierre's glance did not meet his own. Instead, he turned away and his veined, bony hands began slowly to fold up the paper.

"You have seen something," he said, "that no Indian knows I have. I counsel you to say no word of it, my son."

He replaced the map in the chest and turned the key in the lock once more. They talked for a few minutes—about the hard winter and the lack of food. Then, as Dave was about to depart, the priest held up his hand in the sign of benediction. There was a ghost of a smile on his lined face as he spoke the Abenaki words—"May the good spirits go with you when you make your journey, my son."

XVII

WALKING away from the priest's house, Dave hardly noticed where he was going. Excitement gripped him. He had to get off somewhere by himself and think. After a few minutes he found his snowshoes had carried him out of the village and into the forest. There, in the hush of the winter woods, he could begin to sort out the practical ideas from the wild and foolish ones and see more clearly what was to be done.

There was no question of what Father Pierre had in mind when he showed him the map. The priest was doing what he could to help him escape. But what the good Father did not know was that Dave had no intention of going without Nancy.

The boy knew any attempt he made now, in the deep snow, would end in failure even if he tried it alone. They must wait for spring, when they could go by canoe. The priest had given him a secret that few of the Indians knew

—the fact that by carrying across one range of hills there was a water route all the way to the St. John.

He was strong, and a good paddler. With enough food he believed he could do it. His only doubts were about Nancy. Then he remembered the whalebone toughness she had shown on the long trip from the Connecticut and he grinned to himself. Nancy, he thought, would probably outlast him, no matter what hardships they encountered.

His conscience troubled him a little when he thought of the other two prisoners, but he knew neither of them could possibly stand such a journey. Josh Boles was clumsy, a glutton and a chronic whiner. The braves despised him and he had been given squaw's work to do. Dave had seen little of Judith Gray that winter, but he knew she had grown more and more feeble—a woman sick in body and mind. Tragic as her case was, he would be forced to leave her out of his planning.

How they were to collect enough food and how they could get away without being seen were problems he would have to face when the time came. Meanwhile, there was nothing to do but wait.

Chilled from standing there in the snow, he shook himself, thrashed his arms and hurried on to make the rounds of the snares. With the frozen bodies of two rabbits to explain his absence, he returned to the cabin and found Nequanis preparing to cook supper.

"How much longer will winter last?" the white boy asked as he warmed his numb hands at the fire.

"Two more moons, or perhaps longer, before the ice goes out of the river," Nequanis answered. "But why does my brother wish to know?"

Dave tried to sound casual. "No reason," he said, "except that my body is still soft. I have not been hardened to so much cold and snow as my Indian brother has."

Two months. That would mean the first of May at the earliest. He wondered how he could wait so long.

.   .   .   .

It was several days before Dave found an opportunity to see Nancy alone. A hole had been chopped through the ice near the riverbank, and the squaws went there to fill their earthen pots and iron kettles with water. Each morning two or three inches of new ice had to be broken away, but it was better than using melted snow.

Carrying water for their bachelor quarters was one of Dave's chores. The first time he encountered Nancy on the same errand, after his talk with Father Pierre, there were two or three Indian women around the water hole. All he could do was say hello to the girl and ask her to come there early the next day, for he never could be quite sure how much English the squaws understood.

That night it began snowing again and by dawn there was a blizzard so fierce that a man could hardly stand up in the blast. It was two whole days before they were able to dig out and return to the normal routine.

Dave rose in the dark that third morning, took the kettle and the ax, and set off across the drifts to the river. He had dug away the snow above the water hole and was starting to chop into the ice when Nancy came down the bank. She had her own snowshoes now, and the hood of her deerskin jacket was lined with the pelt of the fisher he had given her. The dark fur made a frame for her yellow hair and bright eyes and her cheeks, red as apples in the cold.

"Gosh, Nance," he told her admiringly, "you're pretty as a picture!"

The youngster tossed her head. "You mean you got me up this early just to pay me compliments?" she asked.

"No." His voice was sober. "I've got some real news. You and I are going to get away from here, Nancy."

He told her the whole story while she listened, lips parted and eyes shining.

"Why can't we go right now?" she asked, breathlessly. "I could get some corn for us to eat. I'm pretty good on snow-shoes, you know."

Dave shook his head. "We'd leave tracks that any Indian could follow blindfolded," he told her. "And we couldn't travel fast enough with the heavy packs we'd have to carry. No, Nance, we'll just have to stand it till spring. But I wanted you to know, so we can be ready."

They discussed the matter further while Dave cut through the ice and filled Nancy's kettle and his own. The girl thought she could get a little extra corn whenever she was sent to the storehouse, and hide it in a safe place. After some thought Dave decided against her idea.

"Suppose somebody found it," he said. "They'd figure

we were planning something and we'd be watched every minute. No, we'd better wait till we're ready to start, and act as if we were going to stay right on here and turn Abenaki."

They were interrupted by the arrival of several squaws who shouted with delight when they found the white boy had done all the hard work. That ended his talk with Nancy, but he contrived to see her several times during the weeks that followed, arranging their meetings so that they always appeared to be accidental.

There was a brief thaw in March, but after it the winter shut down more bitterly than ever. Then came April and a bright sun. The snow began melting and the sap stirred in the trees. At Dave's suggestion, he and Nequanis tapped a few sugar maples. But there weren't enough buckets available to collect much sap, and when they boiled it off, they had only a pound or two of sugar to show for their work. The taste of it made Dave more homesick than he had been at any time since his capture. Nequanis was sick, too, but in another way. Unused to sweets, he gobbled half a pound of maple sugar without stopping, and his stomach couldn't stand it. After that he made a wry face whenever he passed a maple tree.

The days were longer now, and the sun higher in the sky. One morning there came a soft south wind that ate into the banks of snow and sent streams of water flowing down the hills. The river groaned all night, straining at its bonds of ice. The next day there were great cracks in the surface, and through them the flood water boiled up angrily.

Dave heard a sound of wild, distant music and saw Nequanis pointing at the sky. Far up in the blue a cluster of pin-point dots made a pattern like an arrowhead, moving steadily in one direction. The geese were flying north.

The Indian boy lifted his arms and chanted a formal greeting to the great birds. "You have lighted the fires of the sun," he sang. "You have tied up the neck of the sack from which the snow feathers fall. The warm winds follow you. The season of corn-planting—the time of hunting and of fighting—is close at hand."

"And the season of traveling," Dave thought to himself. Behind them at that moment there was a booming noise like a cannon shot. Whirling about, they saw a huge section of the river's ice tilt upward as the water surged out from under its edge.

"This is it," cried Nequanis. "This is the breaking up of the ice!" And they ran to join the crowd of Indians gathering along the riverbank.

All that day and night the thunder of the cracking ice continued. Great pieces, twenty or thirty feet across and a yard thick, would break loose and go whirling away downstream. At the rapids a mile below the town a dozen floes piled on top of one another and formed a dam of ice that backed the flood halfway up the bank. For a while the whole village was threatened, but the jam burst at last with an ear-splitting roar. By noon of the second day the river was running free.

THE INDIAN BOY LIFTED HIS ARMS AND CHANTED A FORMAL
GREETING TO THE GREAT BIRDS

Spring had its setbacks after that, but the real winter had ended. In spite of freezing mornings and occasional light snowfalls, Dave could see the season advancing day by day. Fed by melting drifts, the river was still too high for comfortable travel, but the boy spent hours wondering how he could get a canoe when the time came.

One morning—it must have been the first week in May— there was a commotion in the village. They heard shouts while they were cooking breakfast, and a moment later Matawassie came running to their cabin.

"The white woman prisoner is gone," he panted. "She took a knife and a little corn and went out in the night. The chief is sending all the warriors to hunt for her."

By the time they finished their hasty meal the search was being organized. By ones and twos, the braves started to fan outward from the village. Nequanis and Dave were sent northwestward along the riverbank toward the St. Lawrence. The ground was soft and wet but they found no tracks to indicate that Judith Gray had come that way.

After an hour or more they reached a high, wooded bluff that overlooked the great river. From the top they could see its waters stretching away like a sea, and the mountains of the farther shore were no more than a blue shadow on the horizon.

"Look," said Nequanis, pointing to the southwest. Dave shaded his eyes with his hand and made out a sail, moving toward them, half a mile out from the southern shore. It was a sloop-rigged craft of about ten tons' burden, he judged.

"A wind-canoe of the French," Nequanis said. "They may be coming to visit our town. We must go back and tell Maranoquid what we have seen."

Most of the warriors had returned to the village when the boys got there. The search was over. The body of Judith Gray had been found, not five miles away, at the bottom of a ravine. The fall from its edge, in the dark, had broken her neck.

Dave was badly shaken by the news, but Nequanis merely shrugged. "She was worth nothing," he said callously. "It would have been better if Bemokis had taken her scalp in the beginning."

The white boy's anger flared at the words, but he clenched his teeth and held back the hot reply that was on his tongue. This was no time to remind Nequanis that he, too, was a captive and might be thinking of escape.

They made their way to the chief's lodge, and the Indian boy reported the sighting of the French sloop.

"It is well," said Maranoquid. "I will send scouts to find out if they come up the River of the Wolves."

He began the painting of his face and gave orders that the other braves should also prepare to receive visitors.

By midafternoon the village was in readiness. A runner had come in with the news that a canoe was on its way up the river, paddled by four Algonquins and carrying a French officer. A few minutes later the sound of a musket shot signaled their approach.

The women swarmed down to the water's edge to help the newcomers ashore. Dave, waiting at the top of the bank with the warriors, was glad to see that Nancy was not among the squaws who formed the welcoming party. If this Frenchman was buying prisoners, the safest thing for the white girl was to keep out of sight.

As it turned out, the officer's errand was quite different. He was a brisk, wiry little man with bristling mustaches and a leathery skin. After greeting Maranoquid with proper ceremony, he came quickly to the point. The Great White Father across the sea, he told them, was sending strong armies to defeat the vile Bostonnais. There would be glorious fighting in the coming summer on Lake Champlain. They would throw the English out of Ticonderoga and Crown Point. Many scalps would be taken. The Great White Father graciously invited his children, the Abenakis, to share in the victory and its rewards. How many warriors would the great Chief Maranoquid send?

In answer, Maranoquid passed the pipe about the circle, then rose and made a leisurely speech. The Abenakis, he assured the officer, were delighted at the honor shown them by the Great White Father. As the greatest fighters among all the Indian tribes—and here he cast a scornful glance at the four scowling Algonquins—they would certainly welcome the opportunity to enter this new campaign. But what, he wanted to know, were the rewards that had been mentioned?

The Frenchman was ready for that question. Three months' provisions, he replied, with a new musket, powder and ball for each brave, and a quarter-keg of brandy apiece when the victory was won.

A murmur of approval from the gathering showed that he had hit the mark. Again the chief rose.

"When," he asked, "would our party of warriors be required to start?"

"Five days from now," the officer replied. "The men of all the Canadian tribes will assemble at Quebec in ten days' time. There they will be given their guns and their supplies. The main army will follow them immediately to Lake St. Pierre and up the Richelieu to Champlain."

The council dragged on for hours, as one warrior after another rose and voiced his opinion. Only two or three of the old men were against accepting the summons. The main body of braves, led by Bemokis, was solidly in favor of going. When everyone had said his say, Maranoquid addressed the French soldier again.

"This is a long campaign," he said, "and we are doing the White Father a great favor by taking part in it. Before our young men make this journey we would like to hold a feast. Does the French Chief have a sample of this brandy in his wind-canoe, so that we can tell whether it is of good quality?"

The officer said he happened to have a small barrel of it aboard the sloop, now anchored at the mouth of the river.

He would return with it at this time tomorrow if he had Maranoquid's promise of forty braves.

The pledge was promptly given and the visitors got back into their canoe.

"Until tomorrow!" the Frenchman called as he waved farewell.

NEQUANIS was jubilant that evening. He was sure that if forty braves were chosen to go on the war party he would be one.

"It's hard for you, I know, my Brother," he told Dave. "But as you have not yet reached the full stature of an Indian warrior you must stay behind."

Dave nodded, trying to look unhappy. Meanwhile he had been doing some fast thinking. "When will the feast be held?" he asked.

"Not for several days—perhaps the night before we start. There is little food in the village. Tomorrow there will be a big hunt, for all of us must try to bring in game. You and I will go. This will be my last hunting with the bow, for when I come back from the Lake Champlain country I will have my own gun!"

They were up before daylight, going over their bows and arrows, sharpening their hatchets, putting together light packs of food, blankets and utensils. By sunrise the warriors were taking the canoes off the winter racks, patching them where necessary, and applying pitch to the seams. Nequanis found his own small canoe needed no repairs. It rode trimly on the water without a sign of a leak. That was an unexpected piece of good fortune. It enabled the two boys to get away well ahead of the other hunters.

They made the most of their head start, paddling hard to get the winter kinks out of their muscles. The dog, Buck, went with them, keeping pace with the canoe along the bank.

Game seemed to be scarce in the spring woods. They were lucky enough to kill two partridges during the afternoon, but they saw no deer or tracks of deer.

"There is so much water in the forest," Nequanis explained, "that the deer do not need to come to the river."

Buck treed a raccoon that night and they brought it down by torchlight. The animal was lean from its winter fast and would hardly have made a meal for the two of them. However, Nequanis said it was worth keeping, for everything they could get would be needed for the feast.

While Dave was collecting dry wood for a fire next morning, he saw a big, lumbering porcupine going up a nearby tree. He called to Nequanis to ask if the spiny beasts were good to eat.

The Indian boy came on the run. He knocked the porcupine out of the tree with a pole and clubbed it to death.

"Very fine meat," he said. "In the spring this is the only

animal that is fat. He is hard to skin, but he will make the stew taste good."

They got the hide off the chunky body without being stuck by the barbed quills, and it was added to their slim bag of game.

The second day was even more discouraging than the first. Nequanis picked up a deer track but it was many hours old. When they had followed it several miles, tramping through mud and water, they lost the trail completely in a deep swamp. By night the only things they had killed were three gray squirrels and another partridge.

Nequanis was in low spirits when they started homeward next morning. If the others had had no better luck, he told Dave, the fighting men would have to go to Quebec with lean bellies.

"The other tribes will look at us and laugh," he said. "They will ask if the Abenakis have forgotten how to hunt."

They were cheered by the sight of another canoe that they overtook before noon. The four braves in it waved their muskets and shouted boastfully, as well they might. For weighting down the canoe amidships was the body of a full-grown black bear.

It was getting close to sunset when they reached the village. Only two of the other hunting parties had returned when the boys unloaded their canoe. The pile of game on the bank was not very impressive, and one of the squaws told Nequanis that the feast would not be held until the next night—the night before the warriors were to depart.

This was the news Dave had been hoping to hear. As soon as he was alone he hurried off to look for Nancy. He found her in the dusk down by the river where the women were starting to prepare the meat. In a moment he had beckoned her back into the shadows where they would not be seen.

"Listen to me, Nance," he whispered. "This may be the last chance I'll have to talk to you. The feast is tomorrow night. Did the Frenchman bring that keg of brandy he promised?"

"Yes," she said. "It's not a keg, though. It's a whole barrel."

"Good!" he breathed. "Everybody in the town will be drunk by midnight. That's when we must go. Can you get half a bushel of corn and some smoked meat from the store-house?"

"Yes," she whispered. "But I'll have to wait till the last minute."

"All right. Make a bundle of your clothes and blanket. Bring those and the corn and meat to the river as soon as you see the liquor taking hold. I'll be there with the canoe. And eat plenty at the feast. We may get pretty hungry before we're out of the woods."

He grasped her hand for a second, then slipped back into the darkness. That was his last glimpse of her for nearly twenty-four hours.

The town was a busy place next morning. All the hunters had come in and when the meat was assembled there was more than enough to feed everybody. The women labored cheerfully through the day, building their cook-fires, starting the great kettles boiling and cutting up the meat. The braves got their packs together and put on war paint.

Across two logs in front of the chief's lodge reposed the brandy barrel. By late afternoon the men of the village were eyeing it longingly, and it required all of Maranoquid's diplomacy to keep them from knocking out the bung. Finally, when the food was nearly ready, the chief announced that it was time to broach the barrel.

The braves needed no urging. They swarmed around like flies, each bringing a mug or a pot to catch the precious liquid. As the fiery stuff ran down their gullets they gasped, then yelled at the top of their lungs.

Nequanis, already glassy-eyed from the effects of his first drink, saw Dave standing near and pressed a pewter cup of brandy into his hands.

"S-strong medicine!" he hiccuped. "Drink, Brother. It will make you brave as—as me!"

Dave took the cup and pretended to swallow a big drink from it.

"Ah-h-h!" he wheezed, smacking his lips and staggering a little to heighten the effect. "Wonderful! Here, it's your turn!" And he thrust the cup toward the young Indian again.

Back by the fire he found Nancy already eating a steaming piece of bear meat. He got a chunk for himself and joined her.

"The way they've started, it won't be much after dark,"

he whispered. "The squaws will get some, too, as soon as they've served out the food, and they'll be just as tipsy as the men."

He saw Josh Boles sitting close to the biggest stew-kettle, stuffing his mouth with both hands. He had forgotten that the fat white boy would be one who was not drunk. He must be sure that Josh didn't see him when the time came to leave.

The Indians ate, then staggered back to the barrel. Some tried to dance and fell down. Some shouted boastfully about their own exploits, blissfully unconscious of the fact that nobody was listening. The squaws had joined the revelry now, and it took only a sip or two of the strong liquor to send them shrieking and rolling on the ground.

Dave's heart began to beat faster. He caught Nancy's eye on the other side of the fire and she gave a little nod. He stole a glance at Josh and saw that the boy was busy with a shoulder-bone of venison.

He turned away and walked aimlessly past the crowd about the barrel, weaving in his stride as if he also had been drinking. In the darkness near his own cabin he almost ran into the black-robed priest.

Father Pierre laid both hands on his shoulders. "Yes, my son," he murmured, "it is time to go. These poor savages will know nothing until morning—may the good Lord forgive them."

He sighed and turned back toward the chapel. Dave took his bow and quiver of arrows, a small kettle and an ax. He wrapped them in the blanket, together with his deerskin coat and a spare pair of moccasins. Then he went silently down to the riverbank. The light canoe was where he and Nequanis had beached it, with the paddles under the thwarts. He slipped it into the water and crouched in the stern.

Above the straggling row of cabins the flames of the big fire reddened the sky, but below, in the dark along the bank, nothing stirred. He sat there tense, waiting for the girl to appear, and suddenly something cold and moist touched his arm. His startled leap almost upset the canoe before he realized it was only the big yellow dog nuzzling at him.

"Go on, Buck—go home!" he whispered. But the great shaggy head only thrust itself more lovingly against him.

He pushed the dog away with the paddle and took two or three quiet strokes downstream. Then he saw Nancy coming along the bank, bowed under a heavy pack. He swung the bow of the canoe against the shore and she climbed in, stowing her duffel amidships and picking up the bow paddle without a word. A moment later he had turned the little craft and they were moving silently up the river.

The village was more than a mile astern before either of them spoke. Then Nancy's voice came, so low he could barely hear it.

"Somebody's following us," she whispered. "I heard a stick crackle on shore."

A MOMENT LATER THEY WERE MOVING SILENTLY UP THE
RIVER

"Yes," he told her. "I heard it too, but it's a friend, not an enemy. Buck always comes along on our trips. You'll see him in the morning."

The girl paddled steadily for nearly four hours. Then she was so tired that her head fell forward and she slept, huddled there in the bow. Dave was still strong and he knew he must get as far as possible before the Indians roused from their stupor. So he kept going doggedly, taking what rest he could on the smoother stretches and working like a beaver in the fast-flowing riffles.

They reached the first carry just at daybreak and he figured they had traveled twenty miles. It wasn't enough. He beached the canoe and shook Nancy gently by the shoulder.

"We've got a carry to make," he told her. She rubbed her eyes, smiled and sprang out.

"All right," she said. "What do you want me to take?"

He gave her his own light pack and the things she had brought, but not the heavy bundle of food. Then he swung the canoe to his shoulders and set off. Ten minutes later he came back for the corn. They ate a quick meal of the parched kernels, drank from the stream and started again. As they pushed out from shore a low whine sounded behind them. Buck stood there under the trees, looking wistfully after them.

"Come on, boy," Dave called to him. "Come on—only you'll have to do it afoot. We're not taking any more passengers."

The big dog seemed to understand. He grinned and

trotted on up the bank, his red tongue lolling affably.

"I like him," said the girl. "He was the only dog in the village I could pat. I'm glad he's coming with us."

They paddled steadily, logging three or four miles every hour. By ten o'clock Dave was beginning to need rest. His neck and back muscles ached at each stroke.

"We've got a full day's start," he said, "and after the war party's gone to Quebec there won't be any good canoemen left to follow us. If I don't stop pretty soon I'll fall asleep right here."

They hid the canoe in a thicket on the bank and Dave curled up in his blanket. "You'd better take a nap, too," he told Nancy. "Buck'll wake us up if anything happens."

The boy slept soundly till four o'clock in the afternoon. He was stiff when he woke, but ready to go on. Then, with a shock, he realized that Nancy was gone.

"Nance!" he yelled, a lump in his throat, and her voice answered calmly from a few yards off in the woods.

"Buck wanted to show me something," she said. "It's some kind of animal."

Dave seized his bow and hatchet and ran toward her. The girl and the dog were looking up into a tree, where a fat black porcupine sat hunched in a crotch. Dave's arrow brought the heavy beast to earth and he killed it with his tomahawk.

"Nequanis says they're all right to eat," he told Nancy. "If you can skin them, that is."

He hesitated, knife in hand, then decided it was far more

important to get on up the river than to have fresh meat for supper. He cut a piece of birch bark big enough to cover his hand and used it to pick up the porcupine by the tail. They took it with them and launched the canoe again.

May, in that northern latitude, gave them an extra hour or two of daylight, and they made the most of it. By nine o'clock, when dusk began to fall, they had added nearly fifteen miles to the distance that separated them from the Indian town. Here the river was growing more treacherous, with frequent rocky stretches and portages.

"It's no use trying to go on in the dark," said Dave wearily. "We'd be lucky if we didn't poke a hole in the canoe. We'll just have to haul out till daylight and get some rest if we can."

Nancy tried to hide a yawn. "Just as you say, David," she answered. " 'Course, I'm—not—really—tired—"

She pillowed her head on her arm and before he could reply she was fast asleep.

XIX

DAVE slept uneasily at first, starting up at the slightest sound. Then Buck came and lay down beside him, and he was able to relax. He knew the dog would warn him if any pursuing Indian came near.

In the early morning he skinned the porcupine, with such help as Nancy could give him. But the operation took so much time he did not dare stop to cook the meat. There was a long carry ahead. Dave cut two buckskin strips from the bottom of his winter jacket and made a pack harness for Buck. After that the big dog was loaded with the corn sack at each portage and they were able to make it in a single trip.

All day they toiled up the narrowing stream. At sunset Dave climbed a tree and looked off to the southwest. A range of rugged hills stood clear against the orange sky, so near that he thought he could reach them in an hour's walking.

Elated, he climbed down and built a small fire, using a

flint and his knife blade to strike the spark. But when he started to cook the porcupine meat he found it had begun to spoil. He threw it away in disgust. Buck didn't seem to mind the high flavor. He gobbled it down with evident relish while Dave and Nancy supped on corn meal mush.

Any hopes the boy had of reaching the hills the next morning were soon dashed. The river twisted in loops like a snake and its course was constantly broken by falls and rapids. Late in the afternoon they were still struggling upstream, tired and discouraged. Dave was ready to camp for the night but the girl pointed to a placid stretch of water ahead.

"Let's go on till we come to another carry," she said, and he agreed grudgingly.

The smooth water continued for a mile or more. Then, with a suddenness that took their breath away, they paddled out into a little lake, its surface bright as gold in the sunset light. The farther shore rose sharply, up and up, first clothed with forest, then naked with gray rock, to the summit of the ridge.

"That's it," Dave breathed. "The Height of Land! If we can get across it they'll never catch us."

They made camp on the shore at the foot of the mountain, and during the long spring twilight Dave fished from the canoe. He used white grubs that he found under a fallen log for bait, and before dark he had caught three good-sized trout. That was the first really satisfying meal they had eaten since the night of the feast.

When morning came, they were already up, their packs assembled, ready to tackle the climb. There was no sign of a trail but they started out cheerfully enough, Dave carrying the canoe and Nancy and Buck loaded with the duffel and provisions. It was a good thing they had no knowledge of the ordeal ahead of them or their spirits might not have been so high.

The hillside grew steadily steeper and the spruce thickets more dense. Again and again Dave had to put down his burden and cut a pathway with the ax. After fighting their way upward for several hours they found the dry bed of a mountain brook and followed its zigzag course. They stopped to rest at last when Dave thought they must be halfway to the top.

The boy was so bone-tired it was all he could do to force himself to his feet at the end of half an hour. Even Buck eyed the steep pitch ahead without enthusiasm, and Nancy no longer smiled. Her face, scratched and dirty under the touseled hair, was sober now, but determination still blazed in her blue eyes.

Foot by foot they struggled on till the trees grew smaller and the bare rock-faces more frequent. At last they had to climb among naked ledges, gripping at bushes and outcrops of stone to keep from falling. The canoe, which had seemed so light at the beginning of the journey, was a weary load on Dave's shoulders now, and so awkward in shape that it was always bumping against rocks or catching on brush.

Every few minutes they stopped to rest, then crawled on,

panting, their fingertips raw and bloody, their muscles aching at each step.

It was late afternoon when the nightmare climb ended, and they staggered out on a broad ledge at the summit. Dropping the canoe, Dave sprawled face down. He was almost too tired to realize they had reached the top. After a while the sound of Nancy's voice penetrated to his drugged brain.

"David," she was sobbing, "David, if you're not dead, say something!"

He rolled over with a groan. "What's the matter?" he asked thickly. "Is it Injuns?" And he sat upright, staring at her in alarm.

"No," she said. "You lay so still I was scared something had happened to you. Look—there are lakes down there!"

He stood up and his eyes followed her pointing finger. The chain of ponds was just as Father Pierre's map had pictured it—a necklace of blue gems in the rolling wilderness that stretched to the far-away horizon.

They rested until sunset, then started down the more gradual southern slope. Soon the forest was around them once more. Before dark they came to a spring that bubbled out of the rocks, and there they made camp. The cold, clear water revived their spirits, and when they scrubbed their grimy faces and weary arms, it seemed to wash away some of the strain from their muscles. Dave slept like a log that night. When he woke he was very stiff but eager to push on.

They followed the bed of the rivulet that flowed from

the spring, and after several hours it led them down to a larger stream. By noon they were able to launch the canoe.

It was a vast relief to glide swiftly along with the current after the terrible labor they had endured in the last two days. Nancy hummed a little tune as she knelt in the bow. It had no words but it expressed her feelings. Soon the clear, trilling notes of a whitethroat joined in from the woods along the bank. Those were the first homelike sounds Dave had heard for a long time and he brushed his eyes against his upper arm to get rid of sudden, unmanly tears.

Now that they were moving downstream and no longer worried about being pursued, the boy let Buck ride with them in the canoe. The big dog squatted amidships, calmly watching the passing banks. After one or two reprimands, he proved to be a good passenger and kept the craft trimly balanced.

That was the first of five days that they spent on the St. François and the lakes, strung along its winding length like beads. There were stretches of white water to traverse, and difficult carries. But the weather held fair and the fish bit hungrily, so that they managed to eat without using up all their store of corn. Nancy turned out to be a better fisherman than Dave. When they paddled out into the long reaches of Lake Ourangabena she baited her hook with dried moose meat and had a bite within half a minute.

"Dave!" she yelled. "It's a big one! I c-can't hold the line!"

"Oh, yes, you can," he told her. "Anyhow, I can't come

up forward to help. It's your fish."

She set her teeth and wrapped the taut line around her hands till it cut the skin. After a moment the fish broke water and Dave gasped. It was a silvery giant that looked half as big as a man.

"Gosh!" he cried. "Hold on hard. Maybe I can help, after all."

"Don't you dare," panted the girl. "You said it was my fish." And as the line slackened for a moment she hauled in on it as fast as her hands could move.

The battle took nearly half an hour. When it was over Nancy sat white and shaking, but she had boated a three-foot salmon that must have weighed twenty-five pounds. The huge fish not only gave them two good meals but made Buck fatter than Dave had ever seen him.

It began to rain that night and they slept under the over-turned canoe. The downpour continued all the following day. They were wet and chilled to the bone when they paddled out of the St. François into the wider reaches of the St. John. That was on the sixth day after they crossed the Height of Land. On the morning of the eighth day, forty miles down the big river, Dave heard a low, rumbling sound that grew in volume as they went southeastward. The current hurried them faster. He steered the canoe toward the right bank and beached it.

"Must be a big fall ahead," he told Nancy. "I'll go on down and take a look."

A mile downstream the river plunged over a fifty-foot

cliff with a roar that shook the ledges on which Dave stood. He found a well-trodden portage trail, with big blazes on the trees to mark it. No Indian had made those broad ax strokes. White men had traveled through this country! He ran all the way back to the canoe to tell Nancy the news.

They made the long carry around the falls and put the canoe in again where smooth water seemed to begin. Two minutes later they were facing disaster. The river carried them at racehorse speed into a long chute between high rocky banks. Then, all in a moment, they were pitched into wild, white water. Buck gave a frightened jump and the canoe capsized.

Dave kept hold of the paddle and grabbed for his bow and quiver before going overboard. He saw Nancy crawl to safety on a slanting rock as he was swept past. In another twenty seconds he was washed out on a gravel bar in a smother of foam at the foot of the rapids. Choking and gasping, he looked back to see what had happened to the girl, but Buck had already gone to her rescue. She was in shallow water close to the shore, clinging to the big dog's neck.

They found the canoe caught in a tangle of brush a short distance downstream. By some miracle it had been carried past the rocks undamaged. But all their belongings—blankets, cook-pot, one paddle and the precious bag of corn—were lost. Dave had kept his grip on the bow and the paddle. One arrow was left in the rawhide quiver. His knife and hatchet were still fastened to his belt, but his mocca-

THEY WERE PITCHED INTO WILD, WHITE WATER

sins were gone and so were Nancy's.

They managed to gather enough dry tinder for a fire and huddled in front of it. Dave was just beginning to realize the seriousness of their situation. He knew he couldn't blame Buck for what had happened. It was his own fault. And here they were, three hundred miles from civilization, with no food, no shoes, practically no weapons. From the depths of his despair he looked up to see Nancy tugging at the pocket of her wet deerskin jerkin.

"Don't act so glum, David," she said. "I've still got my hook and line."

When the fire and the afternoon sun had dried her garments a little, the girl found a worm for bait and started fishing. After two hours of patient effort she brought a small trout up the bank.

"Here's our supper," she said, trying to sound cheerful.

They cooked it in the embers and it made one good bite apiece for the two of them. Buck would have to fend for himself.

Dave had spent the time whittling a paddle out of a split spruce log. As soon as they had eaten he cut big armfuls of fir tips and spread them on the ground.

"Maybe we can keep warm in these tonight," he told Nancy.

They kept the fire going until their leather clothes had dried, then curled up in their beds of evergreen with the dog between them.

Dave woke before dawn, conscious of an uneasy emptiness in his stomach. He tried to satisfy it with a long drink of river water, but his hunger persisted.

"All right, Nance," he called, putting as much good cheer as possible into his voice. "Going to be a fine day, and we ought to be moving."

She matched his mood, chatting gaily all morning as the river unfolded ahead. Twice they stopped and tried to catch fish but there wasn't a bite. The sky clouded over at noon. With the sunshine gone their pretense of high spirits seemed no longer worth the effort, and they paddled on in silence.

By evening Dave's hunger had become a steady, gnawing ache. He went ashore while there was still daylight and hunted for more than an hour, hoping Buck would lead him to some sort of game. The dog was eager enough but the woods seemed deserted. They came back empty-handed to find Nancy in tears.

"I was fishing," she sobbed. "I had a big one and then the line broke. The hook's gone."

Dave patted her shoulder but he could find no words to comfort her. Things were bad now, and he knew it. That night he twitched and tossed, dreaming of food—no delicacies this time but great steaming platters of meat and potatoes. When daybreak came he had to drive himself to get up. The sharpness of hunger was replaced by a dull apathy. It was an effort even to lift his arms.

"Nance," he said, when they launched the canoe, "we can't stand much more of this and we're a long way from help. Somehow we've got to keep going. Promise you won't hate me if—if—well, Buck would—"

She straightened up, her eyes flashing. "I'm not that hungry," she said. And her hand went protectively to the dog's head.

"All right," he answered unhappily, "I couldn't do it anyhow."

They paddled on, mile after mile. The blade felt heavy as lead in Dave's hands, and sometimes he fought down spells of dizziness. Up forward, Nancy's shoulders drooped but she made no complaint. As sunset neared, a swarm of small, black, biting insects rose out of the swamps along the shore and made their misery complete.

The boy slapped at them with arms that had no strength. At last he dropped the paddle in the canoe and leaned forward, his head in his hands. He didn't know whether to cry or to pray.

It was at that moment that he heard Nancy's whisper.

"Dave!" she was saying. "There's a deer in the water down by that point! Oh, Dave—can't you do something?"

The boy pulled himself together and looked up. Two hundred yards away he saw a big-eared doe munching lily stems near the shore. Without a word he swung the canoe into a little cove and got out, taking his bow and single arrow.

"Keep Buck here and keep him quiet," he said. "If you hear me holler, it means I need him."

XX

DAVE'S weakness and despair were forgotten now. All his senses, sharpened by hunger, were concentrated on one thing. That deer, feeding at the water's edge, was meat!

The boy moved fast but with the perfect silence he had learned in his hunts with Nequanis. His bare feet never broke a twig or rustled a leaf. When he had covered three quarters of the distance he stopped and strung his bow. It took all the new-found strength in his thin arms, but he got the loop over the bow tip.

After a few more steps he dropped to the ground and wriggled forward on his belly. He must get close, for there would be only one shot.

He was not more than twenty yards away when he caught his first glimpse of the doe through the brush. She was still unware of danger. But at that instant there was a flurry of gray wings overhead and the harsh cry of a Canada jay announced his presence.

He heard the deer snort in alarm. There was a noise of splashing, and Dave got to his feet, fitting the arrow to the cord. The animal gained the bank in a bound and for a single second she stood there, looking and listening, a perfect target.

He pulled with all his might and let the arrow go, aiming at the side, just behind the shoulder. And while the shaft was in flight the deer moved. With a sick feeling, Dave saw the arrow strike high in the deer's flank, too far back to cause a mortal wound.

"Buck!" he yelled in a croaking voice as the animal leaped away. There was an answering bark and he heard the dog racing through the woods, but soon the sounds grew fainter and farther away. Dave knew he had failed.

He slumped down on the ground, his hopes shattered and his courage gone. There was a buzzing in his ears and a dizziness in his head. Then, from a long distance off, he heard Buck bark again. Was he mistaken or did the dog's deep voice carry a message of triumph? Once more it came—a short, sharp bark that could only mean "Come quickly— I've got something here."

Dave found Nancy at his side as he ran unsteadily through the woods. They must have gone four or five hundred yards before they found the dog—and the dead deer.

Buck had hamstrung the wounded animal, then made a deep slash in its throat. But, hungry as he was, he had not started to tear the body. Nancy went to the dog and hugged him while Dave began to skin the deer with trembling hands.

"See if you can find some dry wood and birch bark," he told the girl. "We'll cook the liver right here."

.   .   .   .

They rested all the following day, eating as often as they felt like it, but not too much at a meal. Nancy had learned the squaw's method of smoking meat, and when they started down the river again they had fifty or sixty pounds of cured venison, as well as the scraped hide to serve as a blanket.

Spring was coming up the valley with a rush. They saw leaves unfolding on the maple trees and heard birds singing everywhere in the woods. One day they passed two small clearings on the shore. In each lay the blackened ruins of burned farm buildings.

To Nancy the sight meant only one thing. "The Indians have been here!" she said with a shiver.

But Dave had another idea. "Maybe not," he told her. "A few years ago there were a lot of French farmers in this part o' the country. Acadia is what it's called. The British troops came and threw 'em out. I shouldn't wonder if that's what happened here."

As nearly as the boy could estimate, they had traveled down the St. John for something like two hundred miles. It was a broad, majestic river now, bigger than the Connecticut.

Then, one morning they came to another clearing. This

time there was a new log house a little way back from the river, and a stockily built white man was busily filling the cracks with clay.

Dave swung the canoe toward shore, his heart pounding exultantly. Nancy was fairly jumping up and down in her eagerness.

"You'd better stay here," the boy told her. "I'll go up and find out where we are. Maybe we can get some real white folks' food for a change."

As he mounted the bank the man stared at him for a second, then dashed into the cabin and came out with a gun.

"Clear out!" he growled. "Don't want no Injuns prowlin' round here."

Dave's jaw dropped in surprise. Then he looked down at his brown, bare torso and deerskin leggins and burst into laughter.

"I'm no Injun," he said. "I'm a Yankee from New Hampshire. The Abenakis had me a prisoner up north but I got away, along with the girl yonder."

The man rubbed his stubbly chin. "Yeah," he said doubtfully, "I can see yer hair an' eyes ain't the right color, but in that git-up ye sure fooled me. I've got no food here, if that's what ye're after. I'm jest up here for the day, buildin' me a house."

"You mean there's a settlement near?" asked Dave.

"Sure—Fredericton. 'Tain't but about five mile down river. An' come to think of it, there's a schooner from Portsmouth a-layin' there now."

"Gosh!" said the boy. "Portsmouth—that's right close to home! Thanks!" And he raced down the slope to the canoe, panting out the news to Nancy.

They paddled hard all the way to the settlement. The first thing they saw was a weather-beaten, two-masted vessel anchored in midstream, and they wasted no time in bringing the canoe alongside.

A red, bearded face peered down at them and a deep voice boomed, "All hands to repel boarders!"

The words were followed by a chuckle. "Durned if ye ain't white young'uns!" said the man on deck. "What's the idee o' the masquerade?"

"Are you the captain from Portsmouth?" Dave asked.

"Can't deny it," the man grinned. "Cap'n Nate Tucker, at yer service."

"I'm Dave Foster of Dover," the boy told him. "An' this is Nancy Morrison. We're trying to get back home, but we haven't any money. Maybe you know Amos Foster, the cooper. He's my dad."

"Amos Foster? Sure—got some o' his barrels in the hold this minute. So ye think he might be willin' to pay yer passage?"

"Why—I—I guess so," Dave replied, a trifle flustered. Then he caught the twinkle in the skipper's eye and regained some assurance. "Anyhow," he added, "I'm willing to work my way."

"Hm," said Captain Tucker, "first Injun I've had in the

THE "ANNABELLE TUCKER" SAILED NEXT MORNING

crew in twenty years. Well, come on aboard. What about the dog? He supposed to go, too?"

"He certainly is," Nancy answered firmly. "Anywhere we go, Buck goes with us."

The captain slapped his thigh and roared. "I like yer spunk, young lady," he said, as he threw them a rope.

.   .   .   .

The *Annabelle Tucker* sailed next morning with Dave and Nancy aboard. The jovial captain heard their story with clucks of sympathy and great gusts of laughter. All the way down the river he made it his business to see that they got enough to eat. The cook was ordered to outdo himself in preparing fish chowders, fried pies and other good things they had missed in their Indian diet. And by the time they reached the mouth of the St. John they were as sleek and well fed as young porpoises.

The schooner stopped two days at a little fishing village to take on a cargo of salt cod and mackerel, stacked like cordwood in the hold. After that they waited for a flood tide and sailed out across the famous "reversing falls" that barred the river mouth.

A southeasterly breeze gave them a long reach down the Bay of Fundy and through the gap between Grand Manan and the mainland. Then, with plenty of sea room, they cruised leisurely southwestward along the coast of Maine.

The weather stayed fair and the winds favorable. Dave, in spite of his readiness to work his passage, had no regular watch to keep, and he and Nancy spent most of their time talking to the crew, fishing over the taffrail or climbing into the rigging to watch for whales.

Captain Tucker laughed when Dave sighted a spout to starboard and gave a yell of "Thar she blows!"

"We're no whalers aboard the old *Annabelle*," he told the boy. "Ain't a one of us could throw a harpoon if we had to. But they could use an eye like yours down Nantucket-way."

At the end of a week's voyaging they raised the Isles of Shoals dead ahead and the helm was put over to enter Portsmouth Harbor.

The skipper himself accompanied them on the twelve-mile trip up the estuary past Dover Point and into the mouth of the Cocheco. They went in the schooner's whaleboat, towing the little birch canoe astern.

Dave had acquired a shirt and a pair of seaman's boots, and his hair had grown out so that it no longer looked like an Abenaki scalplock. He took Nancy by the hand and led the way up from the landing toward his father's house. A block from the cooper shop he stopped suddenly. A man was coming down the street—a big, tall man with a sparse fringe of red hair hanging below his hat.

Dave turned pale. "It looks like—like my Uncle Jed!" he gasped.

Now it was the man's turn to stop and stare. "Well, by thunder!" he roared. "Is that you, Dave Foster—live an' kickin'?"

The boy took two stumbling steps forward and their

arms went around each other. The explanations had to wait until they reached Dave's house. Uncle Jed dragged him along almost at a run, and his bellowing voice preceded them into the dooryard.

"Amos!" he shouted. "Eliza! Come a-runnin' an' look who I got here!"

Dave's mother fainted when she caught sight of her son and had to be revived with smelling salts. His father, called in from the cooper shop, was so choked up he could not talk. Only Uncle Jed was able to find words.

"I don't blame ye, boy, for thinkin' ye saw a ghost," he chuckled. "Yep, I was sculped, right enough, but I wa'n't killed. Your Aunt Maria got back from McClures' in time to pull me 'round. Sewed my head together, too, so all I got's a scar an' a bald patch."

He grinned at Dave. "The neighbors got up a posse an' hunted the woods for ye," he said. "Couldn't find any sign of ye so we figgered ye'd been took prisoner. But say— who's this young lady? Don't tell me it's the Morrison girl!"

"Yes," said Dave. "It's Nancy Morrison."

Jed's homely face grew sober. "Got bad news for you, Nancy," he said, looking at his hands. "Your pa an' ma was—was killed. Your little brother was hid in the loft an' they didn't find him. Maria an' me have sort of adopted him. We'd be real pleased if you'd come an' live with us, too."

There were big tears in Nancy's eyes but she held her chin up and her voice was steady. "Yes," she said simply.

"I'd like to do that."

Jed Foster, it turned out, was in Dover to get new tools and buy a yoke of oxen. Later that afternoon he talked to Dave about his plans.

"I figger the Injun trouble is about over," he told the boy. "Amherst an' Rogers an' the rest are bound to clean 'em out o' the Champlain country this summer, an' I sort o' suspicion the Rangers might go on up to Canada an' burn a few o' their towns. Leastways, it's bein' talked about. So I'm clearin' forty more acres an' startin' out fresh."

He looked Dave up and down with an appraising eye. "You've put on muscle an' height," he said. "You're big as a man now, an' I'll need a man's help this summer. Pay you a man's wages, too. Thirty shillin's a month an' keep. What d' you say?"

Dave's eyes shone. "Gosh!" he said. "Thirty shillings a month is a lot o' money. It would help me pay Dad back for the passage on the schooner. I'll have to talk it over with him, but I'd sure like to come."

He stole a look at Nancy. She had on a long dress that his sister Jane had outgrown and she looked pretty and ladylike all of a sudden. She was twisting a handkerchief between her fingers, but when she glanced up he saw that her eyes were shining, too. A rosy flush mounted in her cheeks and Dave's heart gave a bump, just as it had when he made her a present of the fisher skin at the door of Bemokis' lodge.

He knew then that nothing could keep him away from

the Contoocook. And some day—when Nancy grew up—

Uncle Jed had gone out to the kitchen and the two were alone for a minute. He went over to her and took her slim hand in his hard brown one.

"I'll come, Nance," he whispered, "and I'll bring Buck, too. It won't be long. You just behave yourself and wait for us."

The familiar, trusting smile was in her blue eyes.

"I'll be waiting," she nodded, and standing suddenly on tiptoe she kissed his cheek. Then she was gone up the stairs in a swirl of petticoats.

Dave had a lump in his throat as he rumpled Buck's furry ruff.

"Gee," he murmured, "don't things turn out fine if you can just stick to it long enough?"

9 781931 177856